A Gun for Silver Rose

A Gun for Silver Rose

RAY HOGAN

Sagebrush
Large Print Westerns

Library of Congress Cataloging in Publication Data

Hogan, Ray, 1908-
 A gun for Silver Rose / Ray Hogan
  p.   cm
 ISBN 1-57490-250-4 (alk. paper)
 1. Large type books. I. Title.

 PS3558.03473 G78 2000
 813'.54—dc21   99-054895

Cataloguing in Publication Data is available from
the British Library and the National Library of Australia.

Sagebrush Large Print Westerns are published in the United
States and Canada by Thomas T. Beeler, Publisher, Box 659,
Hampton Falls, New Hampshire 03844-0659. ISBN 1-57490-250-4

Published in the United Kingdom, Eire, and the Republic of South
Africa by Isis Publishing Ltd, 7 Centremead, Osney Mead, Oxford
OX2 0ES England. ISBN 0-7531-6248-2

Published in Australia and New Zealand by Bolinda Publishing
Pty Ltd, 17 Mohr Street, Tullamarine, Victoria, 3043, Australia.
ISBN 1-86442-002-5

Manufactured in by Sheridan Books in Chelsea, Michigan

CHAPTER 1

THE FAINT, NEAR-INAUDIBLE STRAINS, OF BAND MUSIC drifting on the light afternoon breeze brought Shawn Starbuck to a halt. Leaning forward on his big sorrel gelding, he listened thoughtfully. The sound would be coming from the town—Goldpan, a sign at the fork in the road had stated—still a mile or so on ahead.

Some sort of celebration was under way, he supposed, roweling the sorrel gently and putting him in motion again. Chances were a new gold or silver strike had been made and the settlement was heralding the event.

He was still about three days short of Virginia City, Shawn reckoned, but just precisely where he was in Nevada he didn't know. He'd been in the saddle for days on end, moving first through the towering, timbered mountains of western New Mexico, then across the varying land of Arizona, and reaching, finally, the border of Nevada.

From that point on, all had been desert bleakness with no wild things stirring under the driving sun and only withered grass and weeds and cactus to break the endless stretches of blistered sand. But now, at last, with a great range of mountains looming distantly to his left and various small formations with prominent peaks before and to his right, the country was becoming less hostile.

That, however, was of little consideration. To him the journey to Virginia City was of utmost importance; he would endure any degree of privation to complete it, for there he would find the answer to the question burning

1

in his mind: Was Ben Starbuck dead? If true, the long search was at an end.

Likely that would be the way of it. Shawn had been riding the frontier for six disheartening years looking for his older brother, sometimes drawing close, at other occasions doggedly following a cold trail. In so doing, he had been compelled to halt, at times when money ran low, and take a job in order to continue the quest—an obligation imposed on him by the terms of their father's last will and testament.

At such interludes he would leave a request among the parties with whom he had become acquainted, to pass along the word if they had news of Ben, also known as Damon Friend. Shawn, of course, could leave no exact forwarding address, but by giving the message to stagecoach drivers, freight haulers, drifting cowhands, and the like, and asking them to repeat it wherever they went, an effective if often sorely delayed means of communication was maintained.

News of Ben came to Starbuck in a Mesilla saloon. When he had halted at the small settlement, one not far from the Mexican border, to renew friendship with the bartender, he'd learned that the driver coming in from Lordsburg and other points west had left a message for him.

Arlie Bishop, the marshal of Tannekaw, a town near the Arizona line, and a close friend, had put out word for him to come at once. Ben was dead, the jehu had related to the saloonman, and Bishop could supply the details.

It had come as a shock to Shawn. He was no stranger to death, but he had never really considered the possibility of his brother dying and the search coming to an end for that reason. He had actually doubted that such could have happened, but the bartender could shed no further light on the report, other than to say it was undoubtedly fourth or fifth hand by the time it reached the coach driver and, of course, it could have gotten garbled.

Starbuck had ridden on at once for Tannekaw, found bad luck awaiting him. Bishop, his marshal friend, was found murdered only hours before Shawn's arrival, and no one, including the lawman's wife, knew anything about the message Arlie Bishop had for him. It was a dead end, but Starbuck was certain there was a record of some sort to be found that would tell him what he needed to know, and that proved to be the fact.

Returning from delivering a prisoner to a nearby town as a favor to Bishop's wife, Shawn was handed the sought-for message discovered by her during his absence. It was from the sheriff at Virginia City, Nevada, and it stated, among other things, that Damon Friend was dying of gunshot wounds in a hospital located in that settlement.

The word brought both relief and concern to Shawn. Ben was not dead at the time the message was sent to Arlie Bishop . . . but just when it was received by the lawman was unknown. The note was not dated, and the envelope, which could have carried a postmark, was not to be found. The sheriff at Virginia City—Halverson, he'd signed himself—could have written the message months earlier.

There was no alternative other than to ride to the famed Comstock Lode mining town—now declining according to rumors, since the seemingly inexhaustible store of rich ore was said to be disappearing. But the truth or falsity of such reports was of no interest to Shawn Starbuck; his concern lay only in whether his

3

brother had died, or recovered and was still there, or had moved on.

Should the latter prove to be the fact, it would be no great surprise. Luck had never favored him when it came to an actual face-to-face encounter with Ben, and there had been times when he wondered if his brother wasn't intentionally avoiding a meeting.

Starbuck shifted wearily on the saddle and brushed at the sweat clothing his face as the sorrel picked his way through the low hills toward the town of Goldpan. A tall muscular man with dark hair, too long, and slate-blue eyes, he appeared much older than his actual years.

The lonely, endless trails, all too often marked with violence, the continuing, frustrating quest, the disappointments, the self-denial incurred so that his father's wishes would be realized, all combined to lay their heavy mark upon him, unfairly increasing his actual age and instilling a quiet, cool remoteness that tagged him a loner, set him apart from most men whose friendships he might have enjoyed.

But he gave that no consideration, either. He was a loner by force of the mission thrust upon him, and though he had never turned his back upon anyone in need of help—thanks to his upbringing at the hands of his father, stern, inflexible old Hiram Starbuck, and the gentle schoolteacher, Clare, who had been his mother— he had let nothing swerve him from what he accepted as his duty.

And now it could soon be over . . . finished. He thought absently of what he would do if Ben were dead. There would be legal proof of such to obtain, of course, and to be returned to the lawyer back in Ohio who was handling the estate, but after that . . . what of him, personally?

4

He'd dreamed many times of the life he would build for himself once the search for his brother was over: a cattle ranch of his own, or a place where he could raise fine horses; a wife and family; settling down, becoming a fixed part of the country, forgetting the long, lonely trails.

That hadn't been so bad, he thought. He had liked riding into new towns, following out the dusty roads and dim trails that led occasionally to nowhere, other times to excitement. And there had been the jobs he'd held perforce, for which he was grateful because he'd not only learned the ways of other men, good and bad, but had also, thanks to a desire for knowledge and experience, become expert in several trades and professions.

He would miss all that, should he decide to halt somewhere and put down roots, he knew, so he'd best make no decisions along such lines except after deep consideration—if the choice was put to him. But that was a hill he'd climb when he came to it, although, recalling the message Arlie Bishop had received from Sheriff Halverson concerning Ben, there seemed small possibility of it being otherwise.

Starbuck shifted again on his saddle. He'd be glad when he got to Goldpan. It had been a long, hot day, just like all those since he'd crossed the Arizona border into Nevada—a world of brilliant skies, searing desert heat, alkali sinks, scorched flats, and barren ridges.

Only now was he beginning to see change. Clumps of sage and gray-green rabbit brush were appearing. Scrub junipers created dark, lonely spots here and there, and along the edges of dry creek beds withered dogwoods and willows stolidly awaited the hour when one of the infrequent rains would fill the sandy channel with rushing water and, like the kiss of the prince on the lips of the sleeping beauty in the children's legend, bring them back to life.

It would be good to climb off the sorrel—as beat as was he—find a hotel, engage a room, and after a wash-down or a bath, whichever was more convenient, treat himself to a restaurant meal. Then it would be to bed for a night's rest.

He'd been on the trail for so long that he had all but forgotten what it was like to stretch out on a mattress, sleep with a roof over his head with no need to remain on wary alert for someone attempting to slip up on him in the darkness.

Shawn looked ahead, hand unconsciously dropping to the pistol worn low on his left hip as he reassured himself of its presence. Beneath his leg he could feel the firm outlines of his rifle slung from the saddle, and inside his boot the knife he carried there as a reserve measure pressed against his calf.

The town now lay before him, spread out on a small plain at the base of a slope studded with mines. He'd reached Goldpan finally, and the music he'd heard had to do with a parade that was just getting under way.

The street was a congestion of spectators: men, women, and children in all manner of dress and garb. There was nothing he could do for the time being other than become a part of the crowd until the marching was over. After that he could go about the business of stabling the sorrel and finding lodging and food for himself.

CHAPTER 2

GOLDPAN WAS A TOWN OF FAIR SIZE, STARBUCK SAW as he halted at the end of the crowd-lined street. He let his eyes search along the twin rows of dust-hazed, false-fronted frame structures and the blockier, more solid-looking bricks . . . the Carstairs House. He spotted it, two stories high, at the lower end of the settlement.

Certainly there would be no getting to it just yet. He could see the band, which had apparently been grouped in front of a bunting-draped platform near the hotel, beginning to form a three-abreast column as it prepared to lead the parade lining up behind it.

Brushing at the sweat on his forehead, Shawn swung the gelding about and cut in behind the buildings on the east side of the street. As well move on down nearer to the Carstairs House, wait in one of the passageways until the parade had passed, then cross over to the hotel. The gathering in that area would have thinned by that time.

He heard the band break into a lively tune, reckoned the parade was under way. Cheers began to sound along the sidewalks, rising in volume as he drew nearer to the center of the settlement and the oncoming musicians.

Continuing along the alley, he waited until he judged he was somewhere close to the hotel, and watching for a passageway wide enough to admit the sorrel, he came to one, turned into it, and doubled back along its length to the street.

Stopping at the corners of the two buildings along which he had come, Starbuck looked for the Carstairs. He had halted too soon. It was farther down—he had

7

come out opposite the Lady Luck Saloon, a large, ornate structure, also of two floors, with a wide porch running its street-level width and a balcony extending across the upper. GIRLS, GAMBLING, DANCING & ALL KINDS OF LIQUOR, its sign declared, and from the number of persons crowding its lower area, it would seem to be one of Goldpan's most popular establishments.

Shawn, keeping the sorrel—turned fractious by the booming drums, the blaring brass instruments, and the boisterous onlookers—back even with the edges of the buildings, allowed his gaze to run the town a second time.

Saloons of smaller sizes were everywhere, dozens of them, no doubt all with simple names such as the Blue Front, the Wide Door, Johnson's Place, and the like. The Miner's Hall was a tall, narrow brick structure, but Kennedy's Opera House & Theater was of frame, with a high, square front and sprawling width.

The meeting halls of the Knights of Pythias and the Odd Fellows lodges stood side by side, and near them Starbuck saw the Willow Bud Restaurant, which boasted REASONABLE PRICES. Henline's Drug Store occupied a prominent place in the center of the block, and next to it in quick and narrow succession were offices of a doctor, a lawyer, the land and assay people, and a newspaper called the Goldpan Chronicle.

Except for the Lady Luck, the largest building was Deck Brothers, General Merchandise, although the combination post office, stage depot, and freight dock ran a close second. Hung Fong's Laundry was identified by a crudely lettered board sign into which someone, at some time, unloaded a shotgun. Jenson's Livery Stable was back up the street a distance, Shawn noted. Having located among the assortment of establishments the three necessary to satisfy his need—hotel, restaurant, and the place to stable the sorrel—he put his attention on the approaching parade.

The band, clad in red and blue uniforms, was marching smartly. Behind them came a half-dozen men in business suits—Goldpan's most prominent citizens, without doubt. They were followed by a team of ribbon-decorated bays drawing a light spring wagon that was also festooned but with more of the red, white, and blue bunting that was used on the speaker's platform.

Two men were standing in the bed of the Studebaker, steadying themselves with a hand on the backrest of the seat where the driver, in the military blue of the past war, was holding tight lines on the high-stepping bays.

AMOS LINDEMAN FOR SENATOR . . . The bold streamer affixed to the side of the wagon whipped slightly in the breeze moving through the town as the vehicle drew abreast Shawn.

Lindeman would be the older of the two men, he guessed. Tall, lean, snow-white hair creeping out from under his silk hat, matching beard and mustache, both neatly trimmed; long, swallowtail coat, striped trousers, heavy gold chain swaying gently from the pockets of his vest, he had the distinguished look of an elder statesman as he waved his free hand impartially to the cheering crowd.

His companion was evidently someone of local note. Burly, squat, with a round, florid face, he was wearing a checked suit in which he appeared to find little comfort. A derby hat was perched square on his head, and though his striped shirt was closed at the neck band with a copper button, there was no collar or tie to complete the arrangement, as if, satisfied that the unfamiliar clothing he'd donned was sufficient, he refused to adorn his

9

person any further.

The parade stalled briefly for some reason not apparent to Starbuck, and then there was movement on the upper deck of the Lady Luck. A fresh burst of cheers exploded along the street and he saw a tall, well-built woman step through a doorway into view. She waved to the crowd and to Lindeman and the man beside him. As the pair in the wagon returned her greeting, she crossed to the front of the balcony, and with several saloon girls about her, leaned against the railing.

The dress she wore was bright red and with many tiered flounces. It was cut low at the neck, to reveal a wealth of white skin that contrasted to the thick, dark hair that fell about her head and shoulders and framed her face. She had full brows, a large, generous mouth made rich red by cosmetics; the feathery plumes secured to her tresses by a comb that glinted in the afternoon sunlight formed a sort of perky hat.

"Hooraw for Silver Rose!" a voice shouted above the hubbub.

The crowd took up the cry, and echoes bounced along the noisy street unchallenged by the band, which had for the moment fallen silent. The two men in the wagon bowed to the woman and shortly the parade resumed its slow progression between the lines of appreciative onlookers.

Silver Rose . . . Starbuck continued to study her. She was a handsome woman, he had to admit, and though he guessed her to be in her thirties, she could be older. One thing certain, however: from the acclamation accorded her, she ranked high in Goldpan circles. Like as not she was the owner of the Lady Luck.

"Hooraw for Amos Lindeman!"

The yell went up as if to counter the appreciation

voiced for Silver Rose and to remind all along the parades route of the true nature of the occasion. As the name traveled along the street, Shawn shifted his attention to the two men in the wagon, now directly opposite him. Both were sweating freely, their features shining from heat. The burly individual raised a hand, ran a stubby finger under his collar band as if to release pressure. Lindeman, as befitted his stature, bore up stoically under the weight of the wool coat and trousers he was wearing, but damp places were in evidence.

"We're going to see you get 'lected, Amos!" a man declared as he staggered toward the wagon.

Two bystanders on the sidewalk leaped forward, seized the man—a miner judging by the clothing he wore—and dragged him back into the crowd. Lindeman waved and smiled while sweat ran down his nose and dripped off its tip. More yells echoed from the gathering, and a handful of silver and gold coins suddenly arched through the dusty air and clattered into the bed of the wagon around the feet of the two men.

"That there'll help buy you some votes, Amos!" a voice shouted. "Be plenty more waiting if you need it!"

Lindeman looked down at the money scattered about the floor, smiled, said something to his squat companion, who nodded in reply. The older man then half turned, threw his glance toward the source of the coins, and waved.

"Whatever you got there, I'll double it" a heavyset man in corduroys and canvas cap standing in front of the Lady Luck announced.

"And I'll double that, Amos!" another admirer stated, raising a hand high overhead to make known his identity.

Lindeman reached up, removed the tall, shining hat,

11

and bowed to his benefactors. In that same instant two gunshots flatted hollowly along the street.

The reports were so close together that they could only have come from different weapons, fired from somewhere near Shawn.

He saw Lindeman stagger. The hat fell from his stiffening fingers as he began to slowly sink. Close by, the burly man's face had disappeared into a mask of blood as he, too, began to fall.

CHAPTER 3

THE NOISE OF THE CROWD, THE THUMPING AND BRASSY blare of the band ended simultaneously. For a long breath a tight hush gripped the stunned gathering in the street, and then a loud yell went up.

Starbuck, the smell of gunpowder in his nostrils, fighting to control the nervous sorrel, looked about for the source of the gunshots. They had come from the passageway lying between the buildings just north of him, he thought; or the bullets might have been fired from a nearby rooftop, or possibly a window. It would be hard to tell just where. . .

"Get him! Get the sonfabitch!"

The sorrel reared suddenly on his hind legs. Starbuck threw his weight forward, put his efforts again to controlling the big gelding, saw the crowd surging in about him.

"Somebody get a rope!"

Hands clutched at the sorrel's bridle, pulled his head down. Shawn recoiled as realization struck him. The crowd, believing it was he who had killed the two men, had turned on him.

"Wait—" he began.

"Pull him off'n that horse!"

Starbuck felt himself being dragged from the saddle. He caught at the horn with one hand, tried to draw his pistol with the other. There was no reasoning with the mob. He'd have to fight, use his gun.

"Wasn't me!" he shouted into the sea of angry faces pressing in around him.

He managed to get the weapon out of its holster. It was instantly wrenched from his finger. In that same moment he lost his grip on the saddle horn. His feet hit the ground and his senses rocked as someone drove a balled fist into the side of his head.

"Wait—goddammit—listen to me," he continued, and then, as sudden rage took over, he shook himself free of the clawing fingers and lashed out.

The blow connected with a blurred face. He saw the flare of pain in the eyes as the man fell away. Swinging wildly with both hands knotted, he cleared a small circle about himself, but it was only a brief respite.

The crowd surged in again. Blows began to hammer at him relentlessly, and dazed, he felt himself being propelled into the center of the street. He could see the wagon in which the dead men had been riding, faintly visible through the churning dust, off to his right. The people gathered around it pulled away, and yelling and cursing, joined with the faction manhandling him.

"Get a rope!"

Again the cry went up, this time to be echoed by a score of other voices. Starbuck, fully conscious of what he was up against, fought desperately against the hands locked to him as he struggled to escape. He succeeded in stalling his forward motion, managed to get an arm free, and began to strike out at the men pressing in on

13

him from that side.

"The freight dock—take him to the freight dock!"

Starbuck's free arm was caught, clamped again in the hands of several men. Once more the slow, scuffling procession resumed its way down the street. The dust had thickened, was now a choking, yellow cloud hanging in the lane between the buildings, obscuring their tall facades, streaking the sweaty, distorted faces of the crowd.

"Here's a rope!"

Shawn began to struggle more violently. He was going to hang—die—unless he could break clear, convince the mob that they had the wrong party. But against a hundred or more shouting, enraged miners and other citizens bent on revenge he was finding himself helpless.

"My gun!" he shouted into the ear of the man at his left shoulder. "Look at it—smell it! Hasn't been fired in a week or more."

The miner's expression did not change. Starbuck repeated his words. The man spat at him. The insult sent fury surging through Shawn anew. He managed to wrench an arm free, drove his fist into the miner's jaw, but at such close quarters, with others jamming about him from all sides, he could put no strength behind the blow, and the man, blood trickling from only a crushed lip, merely grinned.

Starbuck flinched, feeling the rough fibers of a rope go about his neck, jerk tight. He shook his head, tried to relieve the strangling circle, succeeded in loosening it slightly.

"Not yet!" a nearby voice shouted. "We got to hang him proper!"

The noose slackened more as someone ran a finger

14

inside it and backed off the knot. Taking advantage of the moment, Shawn jerked clear once again of the hands clingling to him. Fists doubled, he struck out, at the same time kicking savagely with his spurred boots. A solid blow to the back of his head staggered him, sent his senses reeling.

"Goddamn you!" The voice seemed to come from a distance. "Ain't nothing saying we got to swing you from the hoist beam! Can easy as hell fix your clock right here and now!"

"Wasn't me," Starbuck mumbled. "I never fired those shots."

"Say's it wasn't him!" someone shouted from close by.

"What the hell you think he'd be saying . . . that it was him that done it?" The retort was angry, impatient.

"Was him, all right!" someone else chimed in. "Bullets come from where he was setting. Was still on his horse, aiming to make a fast getaway, I expect. Just lucky some of the boys grabbed ahold of him before he could."

"You're wrong," Starbuck protested doggedly as the crowd continued to drag and shove him toward the combination stage depot, post office, and freight dock. "Find my gun—smell it. Been days since it was fired."

"Somebody get a rope?" a voice cut in.

"Already got one around his neck."

"Where's his horse?"

"They're bringing him."

It was useless to fight, Starbuck knew, but he continued nevertheless. He was helpless against such odds. Reasoning with a lynch-crazy mob was an impossibility. But he couldn't give up, and wrestling free once more, he renewed his efforts.

15

Another blow to the head stunned him. He felt the rough drag of the rope at his throat. Abruptly he was jerked backward, went down. As suddenly he was pulled erect.

"Get him up here!"

They had reached the freight dock. A dozen hands lifted Starbuck off his feet, thrust him onto the shoulder-high platform. Overhead he could see the thick crossbeam with its pulley, extending out into the street.

"Tie his hands behind him."

Shawn, twisting, lunging back and forth as he fought to escape the men who had been awaiting him on the dock, felt his arms pulled roughly back, his wrists clamped together, a cord wind about them and pulled tight. The rope once again closed tight about his neck, and he saw its loose end fling up, drop across the beam, and fall, to be eagerly caught by a dozen outstretched hands.

"Wait'll they bring the horse!" one of the men encircling him shouted. "Got to do this right!"

"Right!" Starbuck echoed in a strangled voice. "You're hanging the wrong man! I never fired those shots."

"Come from where you was setting your saddle."

"No. Was from up the way a bit. Get my gun, smell it. Hasn't been used in days."

"Here's his horse."

Shawn looked down. The sorrel was being led through the crowd and brought up to stand directly below the crossbeam of the hoist.

"Make him tell who hired him to kill Amos," a voice from the street suggested.

Starbuck shook his head wearily, glanced over the tightly packed throng: men, women, a few children—

16

some being held high by a parent that they could more easily witness the execution.

"I never killed him—the other man either," he said to the quieting crowd awaiting his answer.

Wasn't there a lawman in Goldpan? Starbuck searched the men surrounding him as well as the people in the street for a sign of a star, could find none. Either the town was without law or its representative was away—or keeping well under cover at the moment.

"We're wasting time."

"Get it done with! Was him, all right. I seen where them bullets come from—he's just lying to save his goddamned neck!"

Again Starbuck shook his head. "Whichever one of you's got my gun, smell it. It'll prove it wasn't me."

"Hell, that ain't proof! You could've figured on maybe getting caught and throwed the gun away."

"Sure—plenty of your kind carries two pistols!"

"Who was it hired you to kill Amos Lindeman?"

The question came again, was taken up by the crowd, once again noisy and unruly.

"I never shot him or . . ."

"Set him on his horse!"

Hands gripped Starbuck, pushed him to the edge of the platform. Someone caught him by a foot, guided his leg. He dropped into the saddle of the sorrel with a solid thud. The rope around his neck was fortunately slack at that moment, gave him only a slight burning sensation; otherwise it would have all been over for him.

"Back off, all you folks," a voice nearby on the dock directed. "Got to give that horse room to move. Now, couple of you fellows hang on to his bridle till we're all set."

Someone seized the loose end of the rope, tied it

17

around the crossbeam's upright, adjusting it to a taut, straight line. The sorrel had but to take a single step forward.

"You're hanging the wrong man!" Starbuck gasped, his voice strained by the pressure of the noose on his throat. He was soaked with sweat and his breath was coming with great difficulty.

"That's what they all say," a mocking reply came from somewhere behind him. "Ain't never yet heard of no killer admitting he'd shot down somebody."

The crowd in the street had fallen back, now formed a thick half-circle around the sorrel. Two men stood at the head of the big gelding, holding to his bridle. A third, a length of leather strap to be used as a whip in his hand, was stepping in behind the horse.

"You got any last words, killer?"

Shawn Starbuck shrugged helplessly and looked out over the gathering, once again quiet. Reasoning—or rather attempting to—had done no good, and struggling as hard as he could, he'd failed, never having a chance against a mob determined to lynch him for the murder of Lindeman and the other man who had been in the wagon.

He reckoned this was the end—the finish for him. He'd wondered many times how it would come: in a shootout, from an accident on a lonely trail some dark night, at the hands of—

"Hold on there!"

Starbuck roused from his bitter thoughts, turned his attention up the street. A small group of men were endeavoring to shoulder their way through the jam of unyielding bystanders. Hope stirred within Shawn.

"What's the matter? What're you stopping us for?" The angry question came from one of the men on the

18

platform.

"Silver Rose. Says he ain't the one that done the shooting. You better wait for her, Pike."

CHAPTER 4

PIKE, A TALL, RANGY, FAIRLY WELL-DRESSED individual, shifted his attention toward the Lady Luck. The one who had so efficiently directed preparations on the platform for the hanging, he now frowned uncertainly, swore.

"How's she know he ain't the—"

The miner who had brought the message pulled off his hat and mopped at his whiskery face with a forearm.

"I couldn't be saying, but she's coming. I reckon she'll tell you."

Starbuck's eyes were on the woman. In the center of a second group, she was hurrying along the sidewalk, hands lifting her vividly red dress to prevent it from dragging in the loose dirt and trash littering the sagging boards. Relief began to course through Starbuck. He took a deep breath, glanced at Pike.

"Get this rope off me," he said. If someone frightened the sorrel . . ."

The tall man shook his head. "Just you stay put till Rose gets here. Maybe she'[l change her mind when she takes a close look. Anyways, I don't see how she could've seen anything."

"Was up on the gallery of her place," the bearded miner said. "I reckon she could see real good."

Pike swore again, glanced around at the silent men ringing him. "If that's so, why'd she take so damned long to speak up?"

19

The crowd was growing restless, murmuring, shifting about, looking toward the approaching woman and back to Starbuck, sitting rigidly on his saddle.

"Get this rope off," he demanded again. "Horse of mine's skittish around a lot of people."

Pike ignored the request once more, his glance remaining on the miner. "You hear me? Why'd Rose wait so long to speak up?" A note of suspicion had crept into his voice.

"Was upstairs—told you that."

"Still hadn't ought to take her this long to come butting in."

"You tell her that, Pike," the miner said acidly. "But maybe you best know the whole story. Said she seen the shootings, started down stairs to stop this here crowd when they jumped that fellow there you got the rope on. Door'd blowed shut and her and them girls couldn't get it open.

"Hollered down for some of us to come up and kick it in. Time a couple of us done that and she got to the street, you jaspers'd already drug this here fellow up to the dock and was putting him on a horse, so she sent me and Joe Evers running on ahead to stop you."

Pike let his eyes briefly touch the woman, now only a few steps away, and then motioned toward Starbuck.

"Take the rope off'n him, but leave him tied and setting there."

Someone moved in behind Shawn, reluctantly removed the snugly fitting loop from around his neck. Starbuck again sighed with relief, let his taut, rigid shoulders fall. There was a stir among the group on the platform, and turning, he watched two men hand Silver Rose up the short bank of steps onto it.

At close range she was a much better-looking woman

20

than she'd appeared from the width of the street, he noted. Well fleshed out but not to the point of heaviness, she had a well-turned figure, and now, bosom rising and falling from her efforts to hurry, dark eyes flashing angrily, she faced Pike.

"You damn near put your foot in it that time, Pike Zeigler," she snapped.

The tall man did not back down. "Everybody said he was the killer," he insisted stubbornly.

"Then everybody was wrong! When the hell're you going to learn to do your own thinking? Sure beats me how you got to be a mine super."

Zeigler stiffened, his lean face tightening with anger. "Now, wait a—"

"No, *you* wait," Rose snapped, and whirled to face the crowd in the street "You people out there are too blamed anxious for a lynching! What's the matter with you? Ain't it bad enough around this town without you ganging up on some stranger and stringing him up for something he didn't do? When are you going to settle down and get some law here?"

"We got Ishmael Shoup," a faint voice stated hesitantly.

"Shoup!" the woman echoed scornfully. "A lazy, no-account passing himself off as a constable! What I'm talking about is a marshal, or a deputy if we can't have the sheriff himself." She paused, glanced to Starbuck. "You all right, friend?"

Shawn nodded, moved his bound hands for her to see. "Can do without this."

"Cut him loose, Tom," Rose commanded, motioning to one of the men standing beside the sorrel. "Then put him back up here next to me."

The miner addressed as Tom and another standing

21

near him hastened to do her bidding. That Silver Rose wielded much power and influence. in Goldpan was evident.

"What's your name, mister?" she asked as Shawn righted himself before her.

"Starbuck."

"Starbuck," she repeated. "I'm guessing rightly that you're a stranger, ain't I?"

He nodded. "Just passing through. Aimed to spend the night."

"And damn near got yourself strung up! Well, you will—as my guest at the Lady Luck, up the street a ways."

"Know where it is," Shawn said. "Obliged to you for the invitation . . . and for stopping this bunch before they could string me up."

"Was close, all right. Hell-raising mining town like this is always looking for something to do, and lynching's sort of their favorite pastime."

"Tinker said you seen who shot down Amos and Caleb Green," Zeigler cut in impatiently. "Who was he? This crowd ain't anxious to give up."

"Well, they can, far as Starbuck's concerned," Rose replied, and put her gaze again on the gathering in the street. "Want you all to take a good look at this fellow so's you won't get mixing him up with somebody else again. Wasn't him that shot Caleb and Amos, and it wasn't one man, was two of them.

"You get a good look at them, Rose?"

"I did. They was standing there in the alleyway between the meat market and Albertson's Hardware Store."

Starbuck threw his glance along the opposite row of buildings. The area indicated by the woman was a few

22

yards above where he had halted to watch the parade.

"Who was they? What's their names?"

Rose shrugged her round shoulders. "Didn't recognize either one of them. Never seen them before."

"Then you ain't sure who—"

"Never said I wouldn't recognize them if I seen them again," the woman snapped. "Got a good look at both, just that they were both strangers to me."

"Killers-been hired and sent here to shoot Amos,"someone on the platform declared.

"About the size of it," Pike Zeigler said, his manner relenting. "Can't figure why they'd want to kill Caleb, however. He didn't have anything to do with politics."

"Expect he just run out of luck," Rose said, tugging at the front of her low-cut dress to better cover the arching mounds of her breasts. "It would've happened to any-body else who happened to be standing up there in the wagon with Amos."

Zeigler shook his head. "I ain't so sure of that. Being head of the miner's union, Caleb was in a position to—"

"He ain't in no position to do nothing now," a voice interrupted from the crowd. "But this ain't finding them two that killed him and Lindeman."

Shouts of accord echoed in the street, and someone asked, "How we going to do that? Been thirty minutes since the shooting."

Rose lifted her hands for silence. The shine of sweat lay upon her cheeks and across her upper lip, but she appeared not to notice. Shawn felt a hand on his foot, looked down. A man was returning his pistol.

"Fellow back there passed this up to me," he said, jerking a thumb toward the center of the gathering. "Claims it belongs to you."

Starbuck, still simmering from the rough treatment

23

he'd received from the town, nodded a crisp thanks to the miner and accepted the weapon. It was his, and after making certain it had not been in any way tampered with and that it was fully loaded, he slipped it back into its holster.

The heady rush of excitement fading swiftly, he was again feeling the drag of the long hours he'd spent in the saddle, the weight of which had been further increased by the struggling he'd gone through in the street as he fought against would-be lynchers. He desired nothing now but to continue with his original plans: to clean up, eat and get some rest, and then ride on to Virginia City that coming morning. Goldpan could cope with its problems very well without him.

"Thing to do," he heard Silver Rose say, "is get busy, round up every stranger in town, and bring them over to my place. When you show up with the right pair, I'll know them."

"Then what?" Pike Zeigler wanted to know.

Rose considered the mine superintendent with narrowed eyes. "You're mighty anxious to see somebody swing. Is it that you've got a taste for blood or are you covering up something?"

Zeigler's features darkened. "I'm wanting to see justice done, that's all."

"You'll get justice . . . when we catch the killers. Maybe we don't have regular law here, but we've got miner's law, and that's just as good. The killers will get a trial, and if they're found guilty, they'll hang . . . but there won't be no lynching."

A murmur of approval ran through the now quiet crowd. Pike Zeigler's shoulders lifted, fell in a sign of resignation as he moved off. Rose watched him thoughtfully.

"Sure too bad about him," she murmured to no, one in particular. "He's a fine man—just gets carried away ever now and then."

Rose turned again to the people in the street. "Wasting good time standing there," she warned. "You want those murderers, best get busy looking for them. Most likely they're still around. I'll be waiting at the Lady Luck."

At once the crowd began to break up, hurry off through the still-hanging layers of dust. Silver Rose nodded to Shawn.

"Want you coming with me . . ."

He hesitated. "As soon go ahead, get myself a room at the hotel like I planned."

"You ain't about to," Rose declared flatly. "Town owes you something and I figure I'm the only one around in position to pay off. Besides, I can fix you up a damn sight better than the Carstairs—it ain't much more than a flea-trap."

Starbuck shrugged, glanced at the sorrel. "I'll have to look after my horse first."

"Harvey," the woman cut in, motioning to a man standing at the edge of the dock, "take Starbuck's horse over and put him in the barn behind my place with my team. Tell the boy I want him taken care of."

Harvey bobbed, said, "Yes'm," and picking up the sorrel's trailing reins, started up the street.

"You can look in on him later if you want," Rose said, "but he'll be all right."

Starbuck said, "Obliged,"and fell in behind her as she headed back across the now almost deserted freight platform.

He glanced toward the center of town. The crowd had split into a dozen or more groups that were filtering into the buildings and disappearing into the passageways as they got the search for the killers under way. The bunting-draped wagon, he saw, had been drawn up in front of a small structure farther down. The sign extending from its facade bore the single word, UNDERTAKER.

Starbuck spurs clinking and feeling somewhat out of place among the miners in his cow-country clothing, brought his eyes back to Rose, hesitating at the top of the steps that led up to the dock from the sidewalk. A man was offering a hand to steady her descent. It came to Shawn then that he hadn't thanked the woman for her timely intervention earlier.

"Like to say," he began, and suddenly rocked to one side.

His gun came up, leveled. Two men, crouched low on their horses, had abruptly appeared at the rear corner of the building beyond the freight depot. Sunlight glinting on their drawn weapons had caught his attention.

He fired twice, the dual reports blending with those coming from the two men. Shawn heard the solid thud of a bullet ripping into the hoist upright just beyond Silver Rose as it barely missed her, saw the gunman nearest the building sag, fall from the saddle. He tried again for the second rider, but he was too late. The man had jerked back behind the wall of the building, was gone instantly.

CHAPTER 5

SMOKE CURLING ABOUT HIM, STARBUCK STRAIGHT-ened slowly as the sudden rush of tension that had gripped him began to ebb. Methodically, he punched the spent cartridges from the cylinder of his pistol, thumbed in fresh loads, and slipped the weapon back into its holster.

Yells were coming from the street as the scattered crowd, drawn by the gunshots, surged back toward the dock. Two or three men who were still nearby, momentarily taken by surprise, broke and hastening to the downed man, bent over him.

"He's dead . . . shot clean through the brisket!" one called, glancing up.

Starbuck felt the woman's eyes on him. He shifted his gaze to her. A wry smile was on her reddened lips.

"That bullet was meant for me," she said, nodding at the hoist timber. "Seems I owe you some thanks."

Shawn's shoulders moved slightly. "Makes us even, I guess. Was about to thank you."

The woman's smile widened, and moving on down the steps, she motioned to the men crouched around the body of the gunman. "Bring him over here. I think he's one of the killers."

Two of the miners caught the man by the feet and dragged him through the loose dust to where Rose waited. The crowd had closed in now and an but encircled her as Shawn came off the platform and took up a stand beside her.

"He's one of them," she said decisively, and glanced about. "Anybody know him?"

There was a general denial. Rose came back to the two miners. "You find anything on him telling who he is?"

"Nope," the older of the pair replied. "Got a few dollars on him, along with a knife, his gun, stuff like that. Ain't nothing with a name on it."

The woman nodded. "Expected that. Jaspers like him

27

hiring out don't carry no letters of recommendation. A couple of you tote him over to Jenkins. Use the money in his pocket to bury him with . . . Rest of you start looking for his partner."

"Can sure bet he's still around, Rose," someone in the crowd said. "They was out to kill you 'cause they know you could tag them for the murders. Best you get off the street and stay under cover till we can catch him."

"Just what I aim to do. Come on, Starbuck," the woman said, and started hurriedly for the saloon.

"Best you keep your eyes open, too," she added as they moved along the sidewalk. "Killer'll be after you same as me since you got a look at him."

Shawn, walking on the street side of Silver Rose, nodded. "Didn't get much of a look. Was a little busy pulling my gun. Did see he was wearing a blue shirt with fancy buttons. Had his hat jerked down low over his face."

"He won't know you didn't see him good," Rose said. "He'll be figuring you did."

Starbuck slowed, allowed others straggling along the walk to close in about the woman. He wasn't worrying too much about himself at that moment; he was where he could see anyone hoping to take a shot at Rose—and him—from somewhere on the street, but to the rear was a different matter; it was only smart to let those following form a shield behind her.

Goldpan was in full search for the remaining outlaw, he noticed. Men in twos and threes, with a hurried intensity, were combing through the buildings, the alleys to their rear, and the passageways lying in between. That there was a large enough force involved in the hunt was evident, but Shawn was having his doubts that the man would still be around.

28

His partner had been killed, and there were now, as far as he knew, many others besides Silver Rose who had gotten a look at him. He could decide it was prudent to pull out while still able.

But, on the other hand, if he had been hired to kill Amos Lindeman, which was the accepted fact, one of the provisions undoubtedly placed upon him by those who were paying for the job would be that they remain anonymous at all cost. Thus it would be most important to the gunman that he leave no witness who could point a finger at him and perhaps start a tracer that would lead to the party or parties behind the scheme.

That was the way the situation should be assessed, Starbuck decided. Rose should take no chances, lie low until the murderer had been caught or there was absolute proof that he was no longer in Goldpan. And Shawn reckoned he'd need to be on guard himself, at least while he was in the settlement. Of course, his plans called for riding on that next morning, and he fully intended to do so. The sooner he got to Virginia City, talked with Sheriff Halverson, and found out what the story on Ben was, the better he'd feel.

"Expect you're ready for some supper."

Starbuck halted at the sound of the woman's voice. They had reached the Lady Luck, were standing at its entrance. He'd been so engrossed in thought while maintaining a steady survey of the street that he hadn't noticed their arrival.

"Matter of fact, I am," he said. The long shadows now stretching across the width of the dusty lane indicated the nearness of sunset. The past hour had gone by quickly.

"Good. I'll have Charlie—he's my cook—fix us up a table."

29

Rose pulled away from him, moved through the open doorway, garish with its red and gold paint, and entered the large, square room. Shawn, throwing a final glance along the street, followed.

Two swampers were lighting the big circular chandeliers that were suspended from the high ceiling by rope and pulley. Each fixture had a dozen oil-filled lamps, and the men were carefully wiping clean the glass chimneys and trimming the wicks before applying a match.

The saloon—complete with ornate, mahogany bar and mirrored back wall, numerous tables and chairs, an area set apart for dancing, and a section devoted to gambling equipment—occupied the front half of the building.

The remaining half, with doors leading into what was apparently living quarters for Rose, the kitchen, and storage rooms on the ground floor, also had an upper level, across which was a gallery that not only ran its width but extended its length to the front of the structure as well.

A stairway led up from a back corner of the main floor to the balcony, and beyond it Starbuck could see a dimly lit hallway off which lay a number of rooms, occupied, he assumed, by the several brightly clad girls who were presently lounging about the tables and at the well-polished counter while they awaited the evening's business.

There were only a handful of patrons, Starbuck noted as he trailed Silver Rose across the room to a rear corner, but the hour was early. Two customers were at the bar, and over at a square, felt-covered table near the chuck-a-luck cage, several men were lolling about, bottle and glasses before them. They were not engaged in any game, were simply passing time with drink and conversation.

"Have yourself a chair," Rose said, pausing at a chosen table placed against the back wall. "I'll go talk to Charlie." She frowned, followed Shawn's glance, still on the men in the gambling area.

"See somebody you know?"

Starbuck shook his head. "Not for sure. Dark one with the sharp face looks familiar."

"Name's Blackjack Johnson. He's my husband."

Shawn masked the surprise that rolled through him. It hadn't occurred to him that Rose would be a married woman—and since she was, why wasn't Johnson out with the rest of the town searching for the man who tried to kill his wife? The woman read Starbuck's mind.

"Expect you're wondering what he's doing setting in here."

"Thought did come to me. Seems about everybody else in town's hunting the man who tried to kill you."

"Well, you won't find Blackjack going out of his way for anybody but Blackjack."

"But if he's your husband—"

"Means nothing . . . to me or him. If the truth was known, he's probably sorry that jasper's bullet missed. You know him?"

"Guess not. Who're the ones with him? Seem pretty friendly—more than just customers, I mean."

"Bunch he keeps hanging around. Not certain what for unless it's protection . . . I'll go see about something to eat." Rose turned, beckoned to one of the bartenders. "Bring us over a bottle and a couple of glasses, Ned," she directed, and hurrying on, entered one of the nearby doors.

When the aproned man had provided the whiskey and

31

thick-bottomed containers, Starbuck poured himself a drink and settled back. All of the girls immediately followed Rose into the rear area, probably to express their pleasure and relief at her escaping the killer's bullet.

The news of the incident would have preceded her arrival by many minutes, but it was evident that it meant nothing to Blackjack Johnson. He'd not troubled himself to even greet the woman when she entered the building, much less show any concern. It was clear that the relationship existing between them was in a precarious state, yet Shawn was aware of the steady, sullen gaze with which Johnson was regarding him: one of resentment.

Starbuck sat up, hearing the door to the kitchen open, and turning, he saw Rose, carrying a plate heaped with food, appear and start toward him. Behind her came the girls, one bringing a small pot of coffee and a cup.

Rising as they drew near, Shawn waited until the food had been set before him and Rose had seated herself in the chair opposite. She smiled as he resumed his place and nodded at the girl.

"This is Chelsy, Starbuck," she said, and then shook her head. "Don't you have another name? I can't go on just calling you Starbuck."

"Shawn."

"He's Shawn Starbuck," Rose said to Chelsy, a slim, blue-eyed, brown-haired girl with a wide, friendly smile.

"My pleasure," Starbuck said, again rising.

Chelsy's eyes danced. "Mine too," she replied, and wheeling, swaggered off with an exaggerated swinging of the hips to rejoin the others collected again near the bar.

Shawn, taking up his knife and fork, started to eat, hesitated, glance on Rose. "You passing up a fine meal like this?"

Shrugging, the woman poured herself a drink. "Once a day's all I can afford," she said with a rueful smile. "I'm near as big as a horse now."

"Nothing wrong with your size that I can see," Starbuck replied.

Silver Rose laughed. "That's a damn lie, but I'm obliged to you for saying it. . . . Blackjack have anything to say to you while I was gone?"

"No. Been giving me some pretty hard looks. He a jealous man?"

Again the woman laughed. "No—leastwise not in the way you're thinking. But if he was—and I was ten years younger—I'd be tempted to give him reason."

Starbuck, enjoying the tender steak, the fried potatoes, and savory vegetables on his plate, nodded. "So would I."

Rose considered him closely. "I think you mean that!"

He grinned. "Always mean what I say. It's the way I was brought up."

"You'd be that kind, all right," she said, and turned her attention to the saloon's entrance.

A dozen men were crowding through. Firmly held by two of them was a prisoner. They halted just inside the doorway, looked questioningly about. Locating Rose, they pushed forward, propelling their captive ahead of them.

"Seems they've caught their first stranger," Rose observed. "You're getting that grub down just in time. They'll be traipsing in here all night—God bless them— dragging in every stray boomer and cousinjack they ran

33

across."

"And the odds are a hundred to one they'll never turn up with the right man," Shawn said dryly.

Silver Rose's bare shoulders stirred. "I wouldn't bet against those odds for sure, but I'm not betting he's moved on, either. That killer's still around somewhere, just waiting for a chance to put a bullet in both of us."

CHAPTER 6

"WE CAUGHT THIS HERE JAYBIRD HIDING IN THAT there shed behind the opera house," one of the men in announced as the group halted at the table. "Claims he was just catching up on his sleeping."

Rose smiled, nodded, looked the prisoner over closely. He was clearly not the man who had shot Lindeman and Green, and later had his try at her, but she did not belittle the efforts of the volunteer posse—all roughly dressed miners—by a flat dismissal.

"Was about his size for sure, Tim," she said, "but he's not the one. What do you think, Starbuck?"

Shawn, taking a swallow of coffee, shook his head. "I'm agreeing. He's not the man."

Tim swore, scrubbed at the back of his neck. "Was for certain he'd be him."

"Fellow with the one I shot was wearing a blue shirt,"Starbuck said. "Had fancy buttons on it—pearl or maybe silver."

Tim glanced around at the rest of the party. "That'll narrow it down a mite."

"He could change, and he will if he's smart," Shawn continued. "Something you can keep in mind, however."

"Like as not he's traveling light," the miner said. "Jasper you shot was. We found his horse, went through the saddlebags. Wasn't toting nothing extra to wear. Expect his partner'll done the same. . . . But don't you worry none, Rose, we'll catch him."

"I'll bet on it," the woman said, again giving the men a broad smile. "Now, all of you go on over to the bar and have yourselves a drink. It's on the house, Harry," she added, glancing at one of the bartenders.

"Might pass the word along to the others to look for a man in a blue shirt," Shawn said as the party moved off toward the counter. "Save you some time, maybe."

"Well tell them," Tim replied, and laid his hand on the shoulder of the prisoner, who made a considerable show of straightening his rumpled clothing and brushing himself off. "It all right if he has hisself a drink, too? Sort of like to make it up to him for us rousting him around like we done."

"Sure it is, Tim," Rose said, and looked again to the doorway.

Another group was entering, and once more it was the wrong man they had in their custody. The woman sent them also over to the bar for a rewarding drink after first telling them of the blue shirt.

Patrons were beginning to filter into the Lady Luck, some halting at the counter, others selecting a table usually with feminine company, or continuing on into the casino, where Blackjack Johnson, his friends still in evidence, was dealing cards. Not everyone in Goldpan, it appeared, was interested in finding the killer of Amos Lindeman and Caleb Green.

"This Lindeman," Shawn began, switching from coffee to liquor, "he a big man around here?"

"Not only here, but all over the state," Rose answered. "Be a hell of a ruckus raised when the word reaches Carson City that he's been killed, and I expect it already has. I sent word to Henry—Henry Deveau, editor of our newspaper—to telegraph the authorities in Carson, let them know what had happened."

"How about the other man—Green?"

"Caleb was the boss of the miner's union, and in a town like this that's a high office. Just about the same as being the mayor."

"You think they intended to kill him?"

"Doubt it," Rose said, nodding to two men passing by. "Like I told Pike Zeigler, Caleb was just unlucky enough to be standing next to Amos. Can figure a lot of the miners will believe the killers were after him instead of Amos, though."

"You think that?"

"Now, I ain't going to say no for sure. Caleb was a hard man when it came to dealing with the big mining companies. Expect there's a couple of them—one's he's stood up against for the miners—who'd like to see him out of the way, but I ain't buying that."

"Was Lindeman they were after, then."

"Yes. There's some mighty big political factions in this state—all trying to get ahold on things. Amos was an honest man, and you can bet they didn't want him around."

Starbuck toyed idly with his glass. "He been the senator a long time?"

"Ain't never held the office at all. Was running for the nomination. Up to now he's been a judge. I remember he—"

Rose broke off abruptly, eyes settling on a slightly built, dark-featured man in a baggy gray suit hurrying toward them through the thickening crowd.

"Looks like Henry's got an answer to his telegram," she said.

Deveau pulled up to the table, bobbed to Shawn, and faced the woman. "Sent that message, Rose, like you told me to. Answer just came back. From the U.S. marshal. Said for us to hold the killer for him. I sent back word that we didn't have him but that we did have a witness who could identify him. Explained you'd got a good look at him but didn't recognize him."

"And?" Rose pressed.

"No answer to that yet. Probably be getting it in a few minutes." Deveau paused, came back to Shawn. He thrust out his hand. "You're Starbuck, I take it—man who shot down one of the killers. I'm Henry Deveau, editor of the paper, the *Goldpan Chronicle*."

Shawn ackowledged the introduction, but before he could voice any comment, Deveau had turned again to Rose and was continuing in his rapid-fire way of speaking.

"Understand the boys've already caught a couple of strangers for you to look at but neither of them was the right man."

Silver Rose nodded, poured some whiskey into her glass, and shoved it across the table to the editor. "Have a drink, Henry. You're running out of breath."

Deveau grinned, downed the liquor. "There hasn't been a story big as this one turn up here since I started the paper. It's going to really put Goldpan on the map."

"Been plenty of murders before this one," Rose said. "Nothing new about it."

"There is when the dead man's important like Amos Lindeman. Expect the story I'll be printing will be headlines in papers all over the country."

"What about Caleb? He's plenty dead, too."

"Oh, I'll be running an account of how he got murdered, too. . . . You from around here somewhere, Starbuck?"

Shawn stirred, having more or less occupied the position of bystander during the conversation. "Just passing through."

"Mind saying to where? I'll need to mention it in the account."

"As soon you'd skip my part in it . . . I'm headed for Virginia City."

"Great place," Deveau said enthusiastically. "Not doing so good now. Ore's running out and the Comstock's not what it used to be. Neither is the town. They've been doing a lot of building since the fire, but way I see it, they're doing it for nothing. Place'll be a ghost town in a couple more years. When you riding on?"

"Morning," Starbuck replied, glancing out into the saloon, now filled with drifting smoke, the hubbub of talk, laughter, and warm, friendly smells.

A man now sat on a stool at the piano and was beginning to play. Several couples were moving out onto the small area reserved for dancing, the women smiling, the men twisting and turning and stomping their feet as though anxious to get started. The crowd in the Lady Luck was now large. There was a solid line at the bar, all the tables visible to Shawn were taken, and a considerable number of men had gathered in the casino, some gambling with Blackjack Johnson, others merely looking on or trying their luck at another game.

"We feel we—the town—owe you a vote of thanks for saving Rose's life," Deveau said, raising his voice to be heard. "Hadn't been for you one of our most illustrious and important citizens would be dead along

38

with Amos Lindeman and Caleb Green. And from what witnesses have told me, it was a remarkable bit of gunplay—your drawing your weapon so fast and shooting so straight."

Shawn refilled his glass from the bottle of whiskey, made no comment.

"I was just thinking—wondering—if you'd care to be interviewed."

"Yes, you're a sort of hero around here now. And being a stranger, folks would like to know more about you: where you're from, where you're going, what you do for a living, things like that."

Shawn stirred lazily, glanced at Silver Rose. There was a half-smile on her full lips. He shook his head.

"No, reckon I'll pass. Nothing much to tell."

"I can hardly believe that. Undoubtedly you have been around the country, experienced many things that—"

"He's not interested, Henry," Rose cut in. "About time you learned to tell the men from the four-flushers."

Deveau shrugged, helped himself to another drink. "Perhaps, but I'll never understand why some people dislike having stories written about them. They're always the ones folks would like to read about while the others—"

"Here comes Jessup," Rose said, again interrupting the newspaper man. "Looks like he's got an answer to your last telegram to Carson City."

Deveau pivoted, his eyes brightening. "Now we'll know what they want us to do," he said in his quick impatient way.

CHAPTER 7

JESSUP, A BALDING, BONY-FACED MAN WEARING A green eyeshade and black satin sleeve guards, hurried up, handed a sheet of paper to Deveau.

"Here it is, Henry," he said, nodding to Rose. "Just come in."

The newspaper editor glanced at the sheet, read down its length, frowned, shifted his glance to Silver Rose.

"Marshal wants you to come to Carson City, look at some wanted posters, see if you can pick out the men who did the killings."

Rose stared thoughtfully, unseeingly at the noisy, restless crowd milling about in the saloon. "Anything else?"

"He says they have a hunch who is behind the murders, and can tie it all together if you can identify the killers. Guess the marshal knows something we don't—like who the killers are working for, if they're the men he thinks they are. He's asking that you come right away."

Rose glanced toward Blackjack Johnson, still at his table dealing cards. "Expect I can. Owe that much to Amos . . . and Caleb."

Deveau folded the paper, thrust it into a pocket. Jessup said, "Reckon I'd better get back to my key. Might be another message come through."

"Yeh, you better," Deveau replied, and as the telegrapher turned away, put his small, sharp eyes on the woman. "I'm not so sure it's a good idea, Rose—not with that gunman still loose and looking for a chance to put a bullet in you."

40

Rose smiled faintly. "You made it sound a few minutes ago like it was my duty."

"Those were the marshal's words, and I never told him about that killer taking a shot at you. I'm seeing it in a different light. It's a two-day trip to Carson, and anything could happen on the way. I don't think you ought to do something foolish."

Rose leaned forward, patted Henry Deveau on the arm affectionately. "Nice of you to feel that way, but I'd be all right. I'm no dewy-eyed schoolgirl."

"What you need is a hired gun—somebody just like them—to ride along with you. Or maybe an escort of a few men would be even better. A dozen or more."

"Turn it into a parade, that it?"

Deveau shrugged. "Guess it would look like that, but you'd be safe."

"Doubt it," Starbuck said. "Would draw the killer for sure—and he could have some friends. Be an easy setup for snipers."

Rose turned to him, features showing concern. No more suspects had been brought in by the local posses, and likely, since it was now full dark outside, the search had been called off until morning.

"Expect you've been around something like this before," she said. "How'd you handle it?"

"Slip off quietly without anybody knowing about it."

"Alone?" Deveau asked in a shocked voice.

"No, have one, maybe two armed men for company."

The woman studied her hands. "Makes good sense. I could leave early in the morning, be miles away from here before anybody knew I was gone."

"Starbuck, why couldn't you be her escort?" Deveau suggested, brightening. "Said you were going to Virginia City—Carson's right on the road. You could

41

drop Rose at the marshal's office and just keep on going. You'd lose no time."

Shawn felt a surge of resentment. There was always something to interfere with his own plans, with the business of finding Ben. It had happened many times in the past, often causing him to fail when success was at hand.

He became aware of Rose's steady eyes upon him, hopeful, pleading, as he gave the idea thought. There was no reason why he shouldn't; he was going that direction, and if they took care to keep their departure secret, the trip could be made without incident.

"Sure, why not?" he said, acceding.

Rose heaved a deep sigh. For all her bravado, she'd apparently had misgivings about her safety. "Thank you, Shawn. I'm really obliged to you."

"Goes for me, too," Deveau said, also relieved. "I—the town would have worried plenty."

"We can use my buggy," Rose said, beginning at once to make plans. "My time of setting asaddle's been over for years. You can tie your horse on behind and do the driving."

"Driving . . . to where?"

At the unexpected question all three glanced around. Blackjack Johnson was standing close by, lean features dark and set.

Rose met his pressing gaze calmly. "Carson City."

"The hell you are!" Johnson said in mock surprise. "What for?"

"The U.S. marshall there wants her to come and look at some wanted posters, try and identify the outlaws that shot Lindeman and Caleb Green," Deveau said before the woman could reply. "Case you don't know it, the same pair tried to kill Rose."

42

"I heard about it," the gambler said indifferently, and ducked his head at Starbuck. "What's he hanging around for?"

"He's taking me to Carson," Rose said. "Just happens to be going that way."

Johnson laughed derisively. "Just happens to, eh? You've come up with better stories than that, Rose, when some young buck took your fancy."

Shawn stiffened, started to rise. The woman laid a hand on his arm, pressed him back. Deveau, face suddenly flushed, shook his head angrily.

"It's the truth! Heard him say before the idea came up that he was headed that direction . . . for Virginia City, in fact. Was me that suggested he—"

"Keep your lip out of this, mister," Johnson cut in coldly. "I don't need you butting in on something that concerns me and my wife."

Rose laughed. "That's a good joke! What I do's never bothered you before, and, anyway, what I do is my own affair. Way it's been, and that's the way it's going to stay." She paused, narrowed eyes filled with suspicion. "Can't figure why you're interested. It didn't bother you none that I almost got shot."

"Was told right off that the bullet missed. No sense making a fuss over it."

"Would be the way you'd look at it," Rose said, drawing the corners of her mouth down in a bitter smile. "You'll be telling me next that you're against my going to Carson City."

"I am. Too risky. But I don't figure you'll pay any mind to me. When'll you be leaving?"

Starbuck endeavored to halt the woman's answer with a shake of his head, failed.

"In the morning. By first light, probably."

"Why so early?"

"Want to pull out without anybody seeing us. In case you don't know it, one of those killers is still loose out there somewhere."

Johnson was silent for several moments. Finally he shrugged. "Well, I don't like it and I ain't in favor of it. Want you all to know that."

The puzzled look had not left Rose's eyes. "Why?"

"You already said it: man that shot Lindeman and Green is still hanging around. Be a fine chance for him to put a bullet in you when you light out across open country."

Starbuck covertly studied Silver Rose. Blackjack had taken her completely by surprise with his show of concern. It was having a similar effect on Henry Deveau.

"She'll be all right," the newspaper man said hesitantly. "Starbuck's an experienced hand with a gun. He won't let anything happen to her."

The gambler nodded. "I'm going to be banking on that," he said, "but you all remember this: I'm against it."

As Johnson abruptly wheeled and doubled back toward the casino, Rose muttered unintelligibly, and reaching for the bottle of whiskey, she poured a stiff drink. Downing it, she smiled quizzically at Deveau.

"Now, what do you make of all that?"

The newspaperman rubbed at his jaw. "Sure a switch-about. I'm wondering if you mean more to Blackjack than we figured."

"Be a cold day in hell when I get around to believing that," Rose said flatly. "Wouldn't alter anything between us anyway, far as I'm concerned." She paused, turned to Starbuck. "We'll pull out first thing in the morning just as we planned, unless you've changed your mind."

"Nothing's changed," Shawn said.

The woman smiled, drew herself upright. "Fine. Now, I've got some things to do: make arrangements for while I'm gone and get ready. You make yourself at home. Everything's on the house, and when you get ready to turn in, I'll have Chelsy or somebody show you to a room where you can do your sleeping . . . Henry, you better get a telegram off to that marshal, tell him I'll be on my way."

"I'll do that right now," the newspaper editor said, and turned away. He halted, looked back at Shawn. "Like to say I'm glad to've met you, Starbuck, and wish you good luck."

"Obliged," Shawn responded, watching the woman move off.

"We'll be depending on you to look out for Rose. She means a lot to this town, and if you feel that you ought to get paid, why, I'll see to it that you are."

Starbuck flicked the man with a shuttered glance. "No charge," he said dryly, and brought his attention back to Silver Rose, moving off into the crowd.

CHAPTER 8

THE LADY LUCK WAS A PLEASANT CHANGE FROM ALL those days and nights of lonely trails. The sounds of voices—laughing, talking, arguing—the smells of liquor, of cheap perfume, kerosene, even unwashed sweaty bodies, created a sort of friendly, warm atmosphere.

Starbuck again let his eyes take in the saloon itself.

45

The swampers had long since finished their chore of preparing the chandeliers, and the fixtures now, back in place at just the correct height above the floor, were filling the broad, smoky room with their glow.

There were pictures on the walls; some, no more than calendar illustrations furnished by liquor distilleries, mine-supply firms, and other enterprising merchants, took on added depth and beauty in the muted light.

The bar itself was a masterpiece. Of rich, dark mahogany, it appeared solid and heavy with much intricate carving, brass trim, and inlays of mother of pearl. Its recessed back section was a gleaming bank of vertical, oblong mirrors polished to perfection. Unimpeded by shelving and other obstructions, they allowed a full reflection of all those who stood at the counter as well as of the constantly moving crowd beyond them. No product of ordinary labor, it undoubtedly had been purchased in some large eastern city where the facilities and the skilled craftsmen necessary to manufacture were available.

"You like some company?"

Shawn swung his attention about. It was the girl, Chelsy. Smiling, arms folded, she looked down at him.

"Sure," he replied, and leaning to the side, pushed back one of the chairs for her.

Chelsy settled onto the seat, sighed, glanced out into the room, teeming with smoke and noise.

"The shootings sure did one thing for us," she said, "made business mighty good. 'Course it's pretty good all the time. Miners are big spenders when they've got the money. This your first time in a strike town—I mean, a place where they've hit it big? You look more like you're from cattle country."

"I am," Shawn said, "but I've been around mines

46

before: Tombstone, Wickenburg, Silver City, a couple of others."

"Wickenburg—I was there once myself. Didn't hang around long. . . . Mind settling something me and the other girls are wondering about?"

"No, not if I can."

"Are you part Indian? Your name. . ."

Starbuck smiled. It was a question he'd been asked many times. "Sounds Indian, and I guess it is. My mother was a teacher who worked among the Shawnee tribe. Liked the word, I reckon, so when I came along she changed it a bit and made it into a name for me."

Chelsy smiled in satisfaction. "I didn't think you looked like one," she said, and reaching for the glass Silver Rose had used, pointed at the half-empty bottle of whiskey. "It all right if I treat myself to a drink?"

"Help yourself," Starbuck replied, and put his attention on the casino, where a disturbance of some sort had broken out.

Blackjack Johnson was standing upright, his features cold and angry as he faced a man with whom he had been gambling and was now having differences of some sort. The four men Shawn had noticed earlier with Johnson, and who Rose had assumed were for his protection, had risen and taken positions directly behind him, making it clear to one and all that they were backing him. The crowd in the casino area had fallen silent and were looking on.

"Just another poor sucker Blackjack's cleaned out," the girl said, noting Starbuck's attention.

"He on the square?"

Chelsy, young, well shaped, and pretty, shrugged. "I suppose so—not that it'd make any difference. He's always right as long as he's got Pete and them others

47

standing by him."

Johnson's customer, realizing the value of being prudent, had turned aside, was walking off into the crowd. The gambler watched the man for a moment and then settled back into his chair. His friends, however, remained in position—a shoulder-to-shoulder line in back of him.

"I'm guessing you don't like him and that bunch hanging around him."

Chelsy met Starbuck's gaze with her level, brown eyes. "And I don't talk about them either. Nobody working here does. It ain't healthy."

"Anything you say stops with me."

The girl sipped at her whiskey, stared at him unblinking over the rim of her glass. "Yeh, I reckon it would. Seen Blackjack over here talking to you and Rose. Why don't you ask her about him?"

"Maybe I will," Starbuck said noncommittally, and glanced again to Johnson and the men behind him. "Fellow on the end—one with the hat on the back of his head—seems I ought to know him."

"That's Pete Dawson."

Shawn gave that thought. "Guess I don't. It safe to tell me the names of the others?"

The girl's eyes flickered angrily, and then she stirred indifferently. "Man next to him, the tall one with the light hair, that's Linus Hawken. They call the one standing by him Chaw—Chaw Sugarman. He tried mining around here, didn't do no good. The redhead's Whiskey Bragg. Done some digging, too, but I guess he ain't much for hard work. Quit it and went to work for Blackjack."

"Work?"

"Sure. Everybody knows Blackjack hired them to

look out for him. He ain't exactly the kind that has a lot of friends. Needs them for bodyguards."

"All four of them? One or two ought to be aplenty."

"Expect it makes him feel like a big man."

"Could be. I'm kind of puzzled about Rose and him. Thought I had them figured out, but now I'm not so sure; I'd like to get things straight before I get mixed up in it any further. Guess you know I'm driving her to Carson City in the morning."

Chelsy laughed. "If there's anybody in this saloon that don't, he's either dead drunk or hard of hearing!"

He should have cautioned the woman to keep their plans quiet, Shawn realized. He actually had tried when she was talking to Johnson, but failed, and then he'd thought no more about it.

"I've been wondering why a couple of Blackjack's bodyguards, as you called them, couldn't be her escort."

Surprise blanked Chelsy's face, and then a hard smile parted her lips. "I keep forgetting you're a stranger around here. Blackjack ain't apt to ever do anything for her. But you best ask her about that, too. I've already done too much talking."

"You've got my word that nothing goes past me," Shawn reassured her, and looked up. Two roughly dressed miners, both well into a bottle, were halting beside the table.

"We're just wanting you to know," the taller of the pair said thickly, "that we're mighty obliged to you for what you're doing."

Starbuck frowned. "Meaning what?"

"The way you're looking out for Rose—that's what! And seeing that she gets to Carson City all safe and sound."

"That lady means a whole hell of a lot to all of us

around this town," the other man declared unsteadily. "Ain't hardly a man, woman, or child in Goldpan that ain't beholden to her for something. We sure don't want nothing to happen to her."

Starbuck swore inwardly, wished again he had cautioned Silver Rose to keep their plans for departure quiet. But the word was out and there was no calling it back.

"I'll take good care of her," he said.

"Fine, fine! Now, you sure you don't want no help?" the tall miner continued. "Me and Artie'll be proud to join up with you in the morning and ride out a ways— clean to Carson if you want."

"Obliged to you, but we've got things already set," Shawn assured the man, and swung his attention back to Chelsy.

The miners bobbed their understanding, looked about uncertainly for a few moments, and then, wheeling, staggered off in the direction of the bar.

"That's a real fancy belt buckle you're wearing," the girl said, reaching over and tracing the engraving on the oblong of silver with the tip of a finger. "That a fighter on it?"

"Boxer," Starbuck replied, glancing at the ivory likeness of a man in the celebrated stance of such centered on the trinket. "Belonged to my pa."

"Was he a champion fight-boxer?"

"Could have been, I suppose, if he'd wanted, but he liked farming better. He'd just put on exhibition matches for the neighbors."

"I remember seeing a fight of that kind. The boxer done a lot of dancing around, but when it was all over, the other man, who was a lot bigger and stronger, was so beat up he could hardly move and his face was bleeding and swole so bad it didn't even look like him.

Do you fight that way—like a boxer?"

"When I have to," Shawn said. "You do me a favor?"

Chelsy smiled. "Yes sir! Rose said I was to look after you, do whatever you want."

"I'm about ready to crawl in bed, get myself some shut-eye, but first I've got to have a little private talk with Rose. Where'd be a good place?"

Chelsy bit at her lower lip, gave the problem thought. "Going to be hard to find, what with all this crowd. And somebody's sure to see you or her going to her quarters or heading for one of the upstairs rooms. Best place'll be the kitchen. Charlie'll be the only one in there, and he's deaf as a post. And he sure won't ever say nothing if Rose tells him not to. He thinks she's an angel straight out of heaven."

"Sounds like a good bet," Starbuck said, and jerked a thumb at the door in the wall nearby. "That open into the kitchen?"

"Yeh—kind of a hallway first. The kitchen's at the back. There's a couple of little rooms that's used for storage in between."

Shawn nodded. "I'll wait in one of them for her. Be obliged if you'll go tell her that."

Chelsy got to her feet. "I'm on my way, and I'll be waiting right here at this table for you when you're done," she said, and hurried off into the milling crowd.

Starbuck rode out a full minute, and then, rising, crossed to the door leading into the adjoining area and entered.

CHAPTER 9

IT WAS A FULL QUARTER-HOUR BEFORE SILVER ROSE came into the narrow hall that led back to the kitchen. Starbuck, waiting just inside the first of the small storage closets, stepped out to intercept her as she closed the door.

"What's the matter?" she asked at once.

He looked at her closely, his thoughts on Blackjack Johnson. "You have some trouble getting here?"

"Nothing to speak of. From what Chelsy said I figured it was important and went out of my way to draw as little attention as possible—that's why it took me so long. What is it?"

"We're going to have to change our plans a bit."

Rose frowned. "Why? What's happened?"

"Everybody around knows when we're pulling out—word's spread all over town, seems. Idea was to leave with as few people as possible knowing exactly when."

The woman sighed, relaxed. "Oh, that. It got around fast, all right. What do you want to do? Call it off?"

"No, no need for that, but I think we'd be smart to leave a couple of hours sooner than we planned."

Rose's full shoulders moved slightly. "That's no problem. I'll have to let the hostler know so's he can get my buggy hitched up."

"Forget it. I'll take care of that myself."

Again Starbuck came in for a close study by the woman. She was silent for a long moment, seemingly listening to the thump and drone of sound coming from beyond the door, then: "Something's happened that's put you on your guard. Was it Blackjack?"

52

"No, just a feeling that we'll be better off if nobody knows when we're moving out—and by nobody I mean everybody, no exceptions."

"I understand, and it's jake with me. What time do you want me to be ready?"

"Let's make it straight up three o'clock. Won't be hardly anybody around at that hour."

Rose laughed. "You don't know Goldpan, Shawn. Saloons here, including mine, never close. Mining towns are like that. High-graders drink and raise hell all night, then go out at sunup and put in a hard day's work at their diggings."

"Can keep from being spotted if we're careful. I remember you saying your stable was out in back of here. Means we won't have to walk far getting to it, and it'll be dark."

"That's right. . . . What about grub? I'll tell Charlie to fix us up some lunch."

"Pass that up, too. I've got a little in my saddlebags. Won't be fancy eating, but it'll get us by for a couple of days."

"Fine," Rose said immediately, running hands down her ample hips. "Missing a few meals will be good for me—can stand to lose the weight. Like to have something to drink along, however."

"I'll get a bottle. Which horse in the stable is yours?"

"The black mare. Be some others that belong to Blackjack and his friends, but the mare's mine. There's only one buggy, so you won't have no trouble finding it."

Starbuck nodded. "Guess that's it, then. I'll have everything ready and meet you at the stable at three o'clock."

"I'll be there," Silver Rose replied, and pointed down

53

the hallway. "Probably best you're not seen coming out of here. Go on through the kitchen. There's a back door that will let you out into the yard. Can circle around then and slip in through the front. Nobody'll notice you when you come in."

"Good idea. See you at three o'clock," Shawn said, and turning into the narrow hall, made his way out of the building.

He was awake shortly after two, relying entirely on his own inner mechanism to rouse him at the proper time. Rising, he dressed quickly, and taking the bottle of whiskey he'd obtained from the bartender after returning to the saloon and Chelsy, he made his way out into the dimly lit hallway that divided the double row of rooms on the Lady Luck's upper floor.

Halted there in the gloom, and well out of sight, Starbuck looked down upon the noisy activities below. The crowd was some smaller, he reckoned, but not to any great extent, and all things were still in full sway. It was apparently true what Rose had said: the miners of Goldpan, and those who benefited from them, never called a recess but continued to work and play the full twenty-four hours of the day.

Pivoting, Shawn moved along the hall to the door Chelsy had earlier pointed out to him, and opening it, he let himself out onto a small landing. Delaying there in the half-dark, he glanced about the yard, saw no one in evidence, and quickly descended the steps. The stable, a square, sloped-roof structure with a water trough in front of it, stood some fifty feet or so away on the opposite side of the hardpack.

Crossing to it, Starbuck entered the totally dark building. The wide door had been open, and closing it to avoid drawing the attention of anyone who might come into the yard, he struck a match, located a lantern hanging from a peg in the wall, and lit it.

Immediately he saw the buggy at the far end of the stable, its black, polished sides and seat gleaming dully in the yellow glow of the lantern. The horses were in stalls to his right, all built at right angles to the runway. He located his sorrel at once, and stepping in beside the big horse, lifted his gear off the partition separating him from his neighbor where it had been placed by the hostler, and saddled and bridled the gelding.

For all intents and purposes he would need only a halter on the big red if he was to be tied in behind the buggy and led all the way to Carson City. But Shawn felt there could arise a time when he would need to quickly mount up and ride, thus it would be wise to have the sorrel ready.

Finished with his own horse, Starbuck left him standing in his stall and moved on down the row in search of Rose's black mare. He found her in the last division, a fine, sleek-looking, well-fed animal that moved nervously about when he hung the Dietz nearby and stepped in next to her.

Calming the black by stroking her neck and murmuring softly, Shawn obtained the harness from its iron hook and strung it into place. Then, backing the mare into the runway, he led her to the rear of the stable and installed her between the shafts of the vehicle.

That accomplished, Starbuck spent a small amount of time checking the buggy, making certain that it was complete and that the whip was in its socket on the dash; then he began to search about for the nosebag. The mare, accustomed to regular grainings and unused to making do with whatever forage was available on the trail, as was his sorrel, would need supplemental rations.

Locating the canvas and leather container, Shawn tossed it into the back of the buggy, dumped a quantity of oats into a gunnysack, and placed it also in the small bed. He had no knowledge of the country through which they would be passing, and accordingly he had no idea as to the availability of water. Such had been scarce, he recalled, during the long miles he'd covered after entering the state, so he'd best take no chances.

Casting about in the dim depths of the squat building, redolent with the smells of hay, leather, dust, and droppings, he eventually turned up two canteens. Examining them as best he could, he determined they would not leak, and first pausing to collect his own water container, he backtracked to the door. Opening it slightly, he had a careful look into the yard. There was no one to be seen, and hurrying to the trough, Shawn filled the three containers, using the water available. It was too risky to work the pump, ordinarily a loosely assembled, rusting arrangement that set up a noisy clatter when the handle was put into motion.

It would be close to three o'clock, he reckoned when he was once again inside the barn. Rose would be coming shortly. Hanging his canteen on the saddle of the sorrel, he moved on to the buggy, and after making sure the corks in the containers were secure, placed them alongside the sack of grain, and then led the black to the head of the runway. He was in the process of tying the sorrel on behind when the faint squeak of the stable door being opened brought him around fast.

He grinned in relief, seeing it was Rose and not the hostler or someone else equally unwelcome at that moment. She had changed her dress to a suit of dove gray and was wearing a bright-red scarf about her head.

In her hand was a small carpetbag containing, he supposed, articles she felt it was necessary to bring.

"Are you ready?" she asked in a cautious tone.

Starbuck nodded, said, "Ready," and handed her up onto the buggy's seat.

Tripping the lantern's globe, he blew out the wick and stepped to the door. Again taking a careful survey and finding the area behind the Lady Luck and its adjacent neighbors deserted, he swung back the heavy plank panel.

"I'll lead the mare until we're away from the street," he said, taking the black's bridle in his hand.

Moving out into the open, Starbuck cut right once they were clear of the stable's entrance, and keeping to the shadows of the trees and brush growing along the back edge of the alleylike area, headed for the north end of the settlement where they could join the road that led on to Carson City.

A door in the rear of a close-by structure—one of the lesser saloons—suddenly flung open, to spill a shaft of light into the darkness. Starbuck halted abruptly, a curse slipping from his tight lips as two men stumbled into view. They were followed by a small, yelling crowd.

The pair immediately threw themselves at each other, wrestling, straining, heaving back and forth as they struggled to land effective blows. The mare stirred nervously, anxiously. Shawn, holding to the bridle with one hand, laid the other across her nose as he sought to comfort her.

The fight was over within only short minutes, both combatants ending up on their knees in the deep dust, neither a decisive winner but calling it off by mutual assent. Motionless, hoping that none of the bystanders would turn, look to their direction, Starbuck waited.

Finally all had gone back into the saloon and the door was jerked shut.

Heaving a sigh, Shawn continued, hearing Rose also murmur a sound of relief. They came to the end of the line of buildings. He slowed, seeing two figures, dim in the pale light of the stars, standing at the corner of the last structure—came to a stop. The men, engaged in conversation, seemed in no hurry, the tips of their cigars alternately glowing bright and dim as they puffed.

Starbuck glanced ahead. Another fifty yards and they would be well out of Goldpan, with the remainder of the night to cover them as they drove northward, but now, with each passing moment, the danger of someone appearing and taking note of their departure became more imminent. And if that occurred, then all would be lost insofar as getting the jump on the killer—or killers—was concerned. Within only minutes, word of their leaving would spread.

Grim, feeling the steady build of tension, Shawn glanced about in search of an alternate course that he could follow. There was none. The steep slope of the hill lay immediately to their right, offering no passage, and doubling back was no solution. They could only wait. . . and hope.

And then abruptly the two men broke apart, one turning off along the side of the building as he walked toward the street, the other moving into the alley behind it and slanting for the rear entrance to the Lady Luck. Starbuck again laid his hand on the mare to steady her. The man would be passing by no farther away than the width of the yard behind the buildings.

Motionless, taut, thankful they had reached the deepest of the shadows, Starbuck waited out the dragging moments. The man, head down, cigar glowing

58

as it dispensed its strong odor, drew abreast. Boot heels crunching in the sandy dust, he passed by—never once looking up.

Breathing easier, Starbuck waited until he had reached the saloon, had pulled open the back door and stepped inside. At that moment he delayed no longer, and dropping back to the buggy, he swung aboard, took the reins from Rose, and hurried on to the road.

CHAPTER 10

STARBUCK KEPT THE MARE TO A STEADY PACE ALONG the gently rising and falling, well-traveled road until the first flare of dawn showed in the east. Only then did he allow the little black to slow and settle, finally, into an easy trot.

Very few words had passed between Silver Rose and him during those first hours, but now, as the air warmed and the land of rolling hills opened up around them, the woman broke her reserve.

"Looks like we've done it," she said, throwing a glance over her shoulder. "Ain't nobody anywhere in sight. I figure that calls for a drink."

Shawn signified his agreement. He, too, was watching their back trail for indications of pursuit, had seen neither rider nor dust. But there was still ample time, and he was saving his congratulations for later—if warranted. A man, or men, in the saddle could quickly overtake a horse and buggy by determined riding.

He took the bottle Rose offered him, had himself a swallow, and returned it The woman treated herself, corked the glass container with a slap of her palm, and sighed.

"Sure goes down good when you're sort of tired and a bit cold."

Shawn let his eyes sweep the country around them. "This the only road to Carson City?"

"Only one I know of. Might be some trails. Miners have been tramping back and forth across here ever since the Comstock Lode was discovered. Why?"

"I'd feel a lot easier if we were on a side road."

"Why worry about it? We got out of Goldpan without anybody seeing us."

Starbuck again swept the horizon behind them with his glance. The sun was up, but a faint early-morning haze still lay, like a gray-blue band, upon the hills and flats.

"Never was much to take things for granted," he said. "This whole thing was an organized scheme to kill Lindeman, put together by some high-up politicians or big-business people who didn't want him elected. They probably have some kind of a deal coming up that they were afraid he'd queer, or maybe they've got something to hide and he was a man they couldn't buy off and keep quiet."

"That was Amos, all right. So damned honest it hurt."

"It would have all ended when they shot him down if you hadn't got a look at the men who did it. And if that U.S. marshal is right, you'll be able to tie the murder to the bunch that hired the killers. Adds up to one thing."

"They can't afford to let me get to Carson City," Rose finished soberly. "Guess I see what you're driving at. Odds are high they'll have another hired gun, maybe two or three, waiting somewhere along this road to finish me off."

"Can bank on it," Shawn said bluntly. "Those telegrams to Carson City about the murders, and you seeing who did them, had to be sent—I'm not quarreling with that. But they worked against us. The people who hired the gunslingers—being high up like they undoubtedly are—probably had the news no more than five minutes after that marshal got it."

"And if the one in the blue shirt back in Goldpan starts after us soon as he finds out we're gone, then we're going to be caught between them."

"About the way it will work out. Big reason why I'd like to get on a side road if there was one, but there's not, and we can't cut across country or follow a trail in a buggy, so we've got no choice other'n to stay on this one and hope we can spot trouble before it hits us."

"I'll watch for dust," Rose said, "both behind and ahead of us."

"Can't figure on that to tip us off—not entirely. Man in horseback won't have to stick to the road, can take the shortcuts, circle wide if he has to. Dust cloud in any direction can mean trouble."

Rose took another swing at the bottle of whiskey. "Well, if it comes, it comes. I'm just mighty glad I ran into you and you agreed to take me along. Want another drink?"

Starbuck shook his head, moodily studied the road beyond the black's bobbing ears. He would as soon not be there at all, much less burdened with the responsibility for Silver Rose Johnson's life. He would have preferred to be on his way to Virginia City with no complications to slow him down, but it seemed that luck inevitably threw an obstacle into his path when he was drawing close to a meeting with Ben.

In this case, however, he was grateful for one thing: doing Rose a favor was not taking him out of his way since Virginia City was but a short ride on beyond the

Nevada capital. About all he could suffer from helping the woman was a brief delay, should they encounter trouble; and thinking about that he reckoned it would matter little if, when he reached his destination, he found that his brother was dead.

"You ever been married, Shawn?"

Starbuck roused at the question. "No. Been too busy."

"Doing what? Just drifting around the country?"

"Had a reason. I've been looking for my brother."

"That why you're going to Virginia City? You expect to find him there?"

"Hoping to."

"I see," Rose murmured, eyes on a broad-winged hawk soaring lazily above the hills. Far to their right lay a short range of mountains with a solitary peak thrust high out of the tumbling mass. "How long have you been looking for him?"

"Coming close on to six years."

"Must be important," Rose said, her voice reflecting surprise.

"It is. Pa died, left a fair-sized estate to Ben—that's my brother—and me. But he put it in his will that things couldn't be settled until I found Ben. He ran off from home after a ruckus with Pa, saying he never wanted to see or hear from us again."

"And you've never come across him in all those years?"

"Got close a couple of times. Once, down in Mexico, I had a look at him through field glasses, but we've never stood face to face."

"What makes you think he's in Virginia City? Somebody send you word?"

Shawn stirred on the seat of the buggy, presently cutting through deep sand and rolling slowly. "Friend of mine heard he was there. Dying of gun-shot wounds. Passed it on to me. Was on my way when I stopped at Goldpan."

Rose had turned to him. "But if he's dying, looking out for me is going to slow you down! You could get there too late."

"May already be. I couldn't find out how old that message was," Starbuck said, glancing around.

His eyes narrowed. Back, in the direction of Goldpan but well off to the right of where the road would lie, he saw a small cloud of dust. It could be a whirlwind, he reasoned—dust devils were common on the desert flats—or it could be riders. He studied the pall for several moments and then, making no mention of it to Rose, put his gaze back to the road before him.

"I'd think you would have lost heart, given up finding him by now," the woman said. "Most men would."

"Got to admit I've had the notion a few times."

"Keep on and you'll waste away your life. Every day a person gets a little older."

"Been told that, too," Shawn said, and drew the black to a stop. "Better breathe the mare—she's been at it steady," he explained, and wrapping the lines around the whip, dropped to the ground.

Moving to the sorrel, none too happy at being trailed, he drew his rifle from the boot and laid it in the bed of the buggy. Rose watched him thoughtfully, but he said nothing and doubling back alongside the vehicle, he checked the black's harness and had himself a good look at the horse as well. The mare was strong despite her small size, showed no signs of tiring. After a time he returned to the seat and took up the reins.

"You think that dust means trouble?" Rose asked as they got under way.

He hadn't realized she'd noticed the yellow pall. "Hard to say. It's somebody coming from the direction of Goldpan—and they're not following the road."

Rose shrugged. "May be nothing. Like I said, there's trails everywhere. Could be a party of miners heading for those mountains you can see sort of east of us."

Shawn nodded agreement, but he doubted what she said was correct. The dust cloud was angling toward them, not for the range of hills well in the distance. And at the speed the riders were traveling, they would draw abreast and get in front of them before the day was over.

But there was nothing to be done about it other than hope it had nothing to do with Silver Rose. He was getting the best out of the black mare without taxing her, and in an all-out race against men on horseback, she would lose.

Riders . . . he gave that thought and felt a stir of relief. There had been only two men involved in the killing of Amos Lindeman and Caleb Green. He had accounted for one; thus it was logical to believe but one remained in Goldpan. The dust cloud was far too large for a single rider—there had to be several horses in the party.

That the gunman could have recruited help in Goldpan was possible, just as it was possible there could have been more than two of them sent to kill Lindeman, but that hardly seemed likely. It just could be, as Rose had suggested, miners going somewhere.

"Trees up there a ways," he said then, pointing to a cluster of gray-green a mile or so in the distance. "Can pull off there, rest the horses, and have ourselves a bite to eat."

"Can use some rest myself—from this hard seat," Rose replied wryly. "Far as eating's concerned, I'll settle for coffee laced with a tot of whiskey."

Starbuck nodded. He was not feeling the need for food himself, but it would be smart to spell the black. Logic notwithstanding, he was not permitting himself to assume completely that the dust cloud was being raised by a party of miners; the mare just might be called on later for a hard, fast run, and he wanted her to be in as good a condition as possible.

CHAPTER 11

ROSE, PERCHED ON A FLAT ROCK IN THE SHADE OF A scrub juniper competing for life with a cluster of narrow-leafed shrubs in a small hollow, dabbed at her face with a bit of lace. The day had turned hot and there was little relief from the shimmering waves drifting across the alkalai flats and sinks across which they were traveling. The land was parched to the point of crusting, and all of the creek beds they had encountered were powder dry.

"I was plain little Emmy Watrous," she said in reply to a question from Starbuck. "Was born in the Arkansas hill country. Nearest town, which was nothing more'n a couple of stores, was called Collin's Grove."

Shawn, finished with portioning out a ration of water to the horses, was leaning against the side of the buggy, his gaze reaching out across the seared land toward a range of mountains. He had lost sight of the dust cloud and it disturbed him.

"Was a hell of a life," Rose continued absently. "Grubbing in the dirt, living like hogs, with nothing to look forward to but more of the same. By the time I was twelve I'd made up my mind I wasn't going to be like my ma, worn out and dying at thirty from having kids and trying to raise them on nothing."

"My pa was a section hand on the railroad; we didn't see him for months on end, and when we did, he'd be drunk. I must've been about fifteen when I took up with a drummer and left home. I learned quick from him what a man wants from a woman, and when we got to New Orleans, I cut loose and went out on my own.

"Stayed around there until all the stories about San Francisco and the kind of money that could be made there in the houses got under my hide, and first chance I got, I teamed up with another drummer that was headed that way, and went with him . . . You looking for that dust cloud?"

Starbuck said, "Yes. Seems like whoever it was pulled up same as we did, or maybe they turned east into those hills. Be seeing no dust either way."

"Probably went into the hills," Rose said, and continued. "Anyway, it took me about six months to get to Frisco, but only about six minutes to line myself up with one of the biggest fancy houses down on the coast. I'd changed my name to Rose, and being young and shaped the way men like, I did real good for myself and the woman that run the house." Rose paused, considered Starbuck with faint amusement. "Me talking plain like this about my life, it shock you?"

"No."

"Well, it's the only kind of life a woman on her own can do any good at. How else can she make money—a lot of money, I mean? And I sure made it. All those miners coming to see the big town, their pockets full of gold and silver they was just busting to spend—I damn quick showed them how! But that wasn't how I got my start.

"Was an old man-up in his seventies, I expect—who

66

took a real shine to me. Had a silver mine over here in Nevada, some mountains called the Pancakes. Time had come when he found himself too old and stove-in to dig, so he hired a couple of fellows to work it for him."

There was a new roll of dust to the south, Starbuck noted as he listened idly to Silver Rose recount her life. It appeared to be moving at right angles to the road they had followed. Someone coming in from neighboring California and heading for Goldpan.

"The old man was good to me, bought me anything I wanted and never asked for nothing more than I expected. Then one night he took sick. Heart was playing out, I guess. Wanted to fix things up so's I'd never have to work in a bawdy house again, he told me, so he willed me his silver mine.

"That's how come I got the name Silver Rose. After I'd give the old man a first-rate funeral, I went there. First thing I did was fire them two sidewinders he'd hired to work his claim. Were stealing him blind. He knew it and told me about it, so I didn't have to waste no time looking into it. Got me a Chinaman and his son and paid them good to do the job for me.

"Figured I could trust them, but I didn't bank on it. I stayed right there with them, day and night, partly to keep an eye on them and partly to keep the claim jumpers away. High-graders coming along, seeing a couple of Chinese working a mine, figured they were fair game. With me setting there with a scattergun across my lap, they changed their minds mighty fast."

Starbuck nodded, smiled politely. It pleased Rose to detail her life, and that she was proud of her accomplishments was evident. But he was only half listening as he continued to ponder the disappearance of the dust cloud.

67

"The Lady Luck—that's what I named it—was a good mine, and before I knew what was happening I was rich, so rich I hardly knew what to do. Then I got to thinking about the saloon business. Always liked it, and from what I'd seen about the way miners blow their cash, I figured it'd be a lot easier way to make money than by digging and worrying about hanging on to a mine.

"So when a couple of shiny-collar jaspers from a big company came along one day and offered to buy me out, I sold. Put the money in a bank in Frisco, made a trip back to Arkansas to see if Ma and some of my brothers and sisters were still there and needing help. They wasn't. Ma'd died and the kids had scattered to God knew where, so I came back and started looking around for the right place to build me a big saloon—one with gambling, plenty of girls, dancing, the whole kit and caboodle.

"Goldpan struck me as just the right place. They'd hit pay dirt big only a year or so before I got there, and the town was really booming. Problem was the kind of place I was aiming to have was already built, although the rest of the town was mostly tents and tar-paper shacks and the like.

"I could've built another saloon, I suppose, but this one was going over big and it was in just the right location, right in the middle of everything. I went to the owner—expect you've guessed who it was—Blackjack Johnson, and asked him if he'd sell. Told me no but that he might take in a partner if I had plenty of cash money and if we got together on his terms."

The black mare had rested; it was time they got under way, Starbuck decided, glancing at the sun. There was no decrease in the driving heat as yet, but that wouldn't

68

come for hours, thus there was no object in delaying.

"I could see Blackjack was taken by me, so I agreed, but I told him the partnership would have to include marrying me."

Shawn, moving toward the mare, paused, looked back at her. "You mean it was you that suggested getting married?"

"I didn't suggest it—I insisted. I wasn't interested in the kind of partnership he was thinking about. I wanted it so's I could take over completely the first chance I got.

"That's how it worked out. In about a year Blackjack got in a bind and had to have some money—a big chunk, five thousand dollars to be exact. He asked me for it. Told him I'd come across if he'd sign over his interest in the saloon to me. Balked at first, but he was in a bad spot, so he finally did and the place was all mine."

Starbuck, readying the black, said, "Expect things weren't the same between you after that."

Rose got to her feet, climbed up into the buggy, and took her seat. "No, they sure wasn't—not that it mattered a damn to me. Only reason I married him was to get my hands on the saloon. I started in then fixing up the Lady Luck—I renamed it that bought a fine bar in Frisco and got rid of the little chicken-dropping outfit he'd had built; added some rooms on and turned it into a real first-class place."

"Surprised he didn't leave."

"No, just hung around. We sort of made an agreement that he'd keep on running the casino and what he could make was his. I didn't need it, so that didn't bother me none, and we got along sort of like two strange cats keeping an eye on each other. But Blackjack ain't ever forgot what I done to him."

69

"Could be a little dangerous for you, feeling the way he probably does."

"Hates my insides, that's for sure," Rose said. "I'm on my guard all the time." She hesitated, then, "Once tried to pay him off if he'd pull out and never come back. He just laughed at me, said he wasn't about to, because he figured he'd get the place back someday."

Starbuck, having checked the sorrel's lead rope and finding it secure, mounted to the seat beside the woman and took up the reins.

"Could take that as a threat," he said as he wheeled the buggy up out of the swale back onto the road, running directly toward a line of brushcovered bluffs a short distance ahead. He understood now Blackjack Johnson's bitter attitude toward Silver Rose and all those who had much to do with her.

"That's how I see it," she said, "and I've done some deep thinking about beating him to the punch. Will you be back this way when you've finished your business in Virginia City?"

"Most likely," Shawn said, eyes on the bluffs. He'd seen movement just beyond the first jutting shoulder of the formation, but it was brief . . . probably a bird.

"You be interested in doing a job for me?"

Starbuck turned to the woman. "You mean kill your husband?" he asked, putting it point-blank.

Rose's lips were pulled down to a hard line. "Just what I mean. Get yourself in a card game with him, catch him on the street, any way that suits you. And if there's a question about—"

"Not interested," Shawn cut in quietly.

"You can name your price," Rose began, and broke off suddenly.

Three riders had appeared at the edge of the bluffs,

70

spurting abruptly into view. Guns ready, they strung out across the road. Silver Rose swore harshly.

"Deals off," she said with a grim smile. "Blackjack's beat me to the draw."

CHAPTER 12

SUGARMAN . . . HAWKEN . . . PETE DAWSON. Starbuck recognized the men: three of the quartet who hung around Blackjack Johnson.

"Don't try reaching for that iron you're wearing," Dawson warned as they approached slowly. "Just maybe'd be the last move you'd ever make. Now, supposing you raise your hands."

Shawn complied reluctantly. He had expected trouble from Amos Lindeman's killer, and possibly others hired by the unknown faction that had wanted the man dead, but not from Silver Rose's husband. But now that he was aware of the situation between Blackjack and the saloon woman, he was not too surprised.

"What the hell you want, Pete?" Rose demanded harshly.

Dawson grinned faintly, dismounted. With Sugarman and Linus Hawken holding their weapons leveled, he swaggered up to the buggy.

"Reckon you've heard the old saying about every dog having his day. Well, I guess you could say this here's going to be Blackjack's day," he drawled, and reaching out, pulled Starbuck's pistol from its holster and thrust it under his belt. Glancing into the bed of the buggy, he saw the rifle, took possession of it also.

Shawn, rigid on the seat beside Rose, watched the two men, still mounted, closely. He would have no

71

chance at all should he attempt to jump Dawson. They could cut him down before he was half out of the seat.

"Like Blackjack to push his dirty work off on somebody else," he heard Silver Rose say. "How much he paying you to kill me?"

"Enough," Dawson replied.

The woman glanced at the other men, then came back to Pete. "Tell me how much, and I'll double it if you'll forget what you came here to do. You won't even have to go back to town—just follow us into Carson and I'll get you the cash."

"Yeh, I'll just bet you would," Chaw Sugarman said dryly. "It'd take you just about two minutes to sic that U.S. marshal on to us."

"You'd have my word."

"That ain't worth much, knowing what you done to Blackjack."

Rose frowned, brushed at the sweat on her upper lip. "Done? I bought him out, paid him off in full. If he's told you something different, he's a goddamned liar!"

"Ain't saying you didn't, only saying you suckered him into marrying up with you so's you could get him by the short hair. Then first time he got hisself in a picklement, you froze him out."

"Not just exactly how it was, but it's close," Rose said. "What's next?"

"Want you to scooch over there to the middle of the seat. I'm going to do the driving," Dawson said, and tossing the rifle to Hawken, laid his hard glance on Shawn. "You, cowboy, best not get any cute ideas. Chaw and Linus'll be riding right behind us. You bat an eye and you'll get your head blowed off. Now, move over."

Starbuck drew himself over to the extreme end of the

seat, making room for Rose to also slide over and create space for Dawson. He was still taut, riding out the moments, watching for an opportunity to make a break, but with Dawson's partners now taking up positions in back of the vehicle, ready to shoot, possibilities were becoming slimmer.

"Where we going?" Rose demanded.

"Taking a ride,"Dawson replied laconically, picking up the reins. Glancing back to see if Sugarman and Hawken were in place, he slapped the mare with the slack in the lines and started forward on the road.

"Ride to where?" Rose persisted. "If you're aiming to shoot us, why don't you do it here and now . . . get it over with?"

" 'Cause that ain't the way Blackjack wants us to do it," Pete said, cutting the vehicle off the established course and striking out across country. "He said we was to fix it so's nobody'd ever know what happened to you. I reckon you could say you're just dropping out of sight."

"And folks will think it was that bunch that had Amos killed that did it."

"Just what he figures. Blackjack's been waiting a long time for a chance like this'n to come along. Worked out real fine. Them two killers don't know it, but they done him a mighty big favor." Pete hesitated, leaned forward and grinned at Shawn. "For such a stem-winding son of a bitch you're mighty tame now!"

"Right time for everything," Starbuck said. The mare, finding the going in the untracked, loose sand hard, had slowed to a laboring walk.

"You scheming up something?"

"Maybe . . ."

"Ain't no maybe to it! Your goose is done cooked,"

Dawson said, and laughed, amused for some reason by what he had said.

"You're damn fools, all three of you," Rose said then. "I can fix you up with enough cash—gold—to keep you in tall cotton the rest of your lives!"

"So can Blackjack. Soon's he takes over the saloon again, me and the boys've got us big-paying jobs. Real easy ones, too, just sort of looking out for him."

"Seems to me you've been doing that right along."

"Yeh, but there ain't been much pay. You been hogging all the money. Be different when it all belongs to him again."

"What makes you think he's going to get his hands on my money?"

"He's your husband, ain't he?"

"Don't mean a damned thing! I've got most of my money stashed away in the bank—two or three of them, in fact—in San Francisco. Can't nobody touch it but me."

Pete swiped at the sweat on his forehead with the back of a hand as he gave that thought, shrugged.

"I reckon Blackjack'll figure it out somehow. Anyways, there'll be all that money coming in at the Lady Luck."

"You're fooling yourself, Pete," Rose snorted. "Blackjack's a loser. He won't ever have a dime, no matter how much he gets his hands on. And there'll be four of you, five counting him, to split it up between, after the bills are paid."

Starbuck listened idly to Silver Rose's fruitless arguing. She was getting nowhere, and whatever fate lay ahead for her and for him was drawing nearer with each passing moment, but try as he would, he could find no opening that would afford escape.

The seat rest and the top of the buggy hid them from Sugarman and Hawken, riding a few paces behind the trailing sorrel, but they afforded no protection from a bullet. He could perhaps suddenly throw himself against Rose and dislodge Dawson from his seat—too narrow for three passengers—but it would accomplish nothing. Even with Pete out of the vehicle and the aim of the pair riding behind obscured, they had only to shoot the mare and bring the escape attempt to a quick halt.

But there had to be a way. He couldn't give in, let it all end without putting up a fight. He still had his knife inside his boot, and the opportunity might yet come to use it, if not while riding in the buggy, when they reached wherever they were going. Rose again brought up that question.

"Where you taking us? Do you know, or are we just riding across this flat?"

"I know," Pete said. "Why you reckon we rode out ahead of you? Was so we could be waiting at them bluffs."

Evidently the dust cloud he and Rose had noted drifting over the land to the east had been the three riders hurrying to get in front of them, Shawn realized. He had thought at the time it might be Lindeman's killer, with recruited aid; instead it had been Dawson and the others, sent by Blackjack Johnson to kill them, but for a different reason.

Shawn was recalling, too, the gambler's words spoken that previous night in the saloon. His concern for Silver Rose's welfare on the trip to Carson City had puzzled her as well as Henry Deveau, but that it was all for a purpose was clear now; Blackjack had simply capitalized on the opportunity afforded him by the U.S. marshal, and laid the groundwork for placing himself

75

above suspicion for her death.

"That don't tell me nothing," Rose said.

"Ought. You recollect that old ghost town east of here, the one that petered out in only about six months?"

Rose nodded slowly. "Yeh—Hangdog."

"Well, that's where we're a' going."

"Ain't nothing but a few shacks . . ."

"Big reason why," Dawson said, and pointed ahead to a low, smooth-topped hill. "We're about there. It's just right on the other side of that."

Rose turned, glanced at Starbuck. Resignation had finally claimed her, and now she had only apology in her eyes.

"I'm sure sorry I drug you into this."

Shawn's shoulders stirred indifferently. "Not over with yet," he said in a low voice inaudible to Pete because of the grating of the buggy's iron-tired wheels in the sand. "What all is there in this town?"

"Nothing. Like I said, it ain't nothing but a few old shacks. Was a strike there, but the ore run out fast. Hangdog hardly lasted long enough for folks to get moved in."

"Can't hear what you're whispering about," Dawson said, "but it ain't going to do you no good if you're aiming to try and get away from us. You've plain come to the end of the line, lady—you and your friend both. Best you make up your mind to that."

"I suppose so," Silver Rose said wearily. "But it ain't right you making Starbuck here pay for my troubles with Blackjack. He just happened to be handy."

"Can talk, can't he?" Dawson cut in. "We let him go, and the law'd be down on us and Blackjack quicker'n a cat can blink his eye."

"Not if he gave you his word he'd keep quiet. He's

heading on for other parts and there'd not be—"

"You're sure great at making promises, ain't you, Rose? Can save your wind. It don't cut no ice with us. . . . Reckon we're here."

They had rounded the low, volcanolike hill, were dropping into a hollow that lay at its opposite side. A scatter of shacks sagged in the driving sun, and as the buggy rolled toward the center of the collection, two coyotes broke suddenly from the farthest and loped off into sparse brush. Back up on the slope a welter of holes, like dark, empty eyes, marked the locations where men had pressed their search for precious ore.

"Climb down," Dawson ordered, bringing the buggy to a stop in front of the largest of the huts. "And don't be forgetting Chaw and Linus'll be keepin an eye on you."

Starbuck swung his legs over the side of the seat, dropped to the ground. Turning, he reached out for Rose, set her on her feet. Still in their saddles, Dawson's two friends, pistols drawn, watched narrowly.

"Get inside," Pete directed, pulling back the door of the shack. "This here's your coffin, in case you ain't figured it out yet."

Rose frowned. "Coffin," she repeated, and moved slowly into the squat, frame structure resting on corner supports of rock.

"Just what I said," Dawson assured her, giving Starbuck a push and sending him stumbling into the building's shadowy interior.

Immediately Pete slammed the door shut, releasing a shower of dust from the walls and ceiling. There followed the dull clink of metal as he closed the hasp and set the peg in the loop.

"Drag up one of them there timbers," he called out to

Sugarman and Linus Hawken. "Got to wedge it against this here door so's that Starbuck can't go kicking it down."

One of the pair evidently made a reply, inaudible to Shawn and Silver Rose, relative to why Pete didn't do it himself.

"I got to get some weeds piled up against the sides of the shack," he explained. "Make it easy to get us a fire going."

CHAPTER 13

ROSE TURNED TO STARBUCK. A HARD SMILE PARTED her lips. "Guess we know now what they're aiming to do."

Shawn, standing motionless in the center of the shack, nodded grimly.

"Like to tell you again I'm mighty sorry I got you into this," the woman continued.

"Sort of walked into it on my own, so don't go blaming yourself too much," he said, listening to the sounds beyond the paper-dry board walls. There was a constant scraping noise caused, he supposed, by the clumps of dead weeds being jammed alongside the structure.

"Hadn't been for me you couldn've kept right on going," Rose said, brushing at her face and neck. The trapped heat inside the airless shack was murderous.

Starbuck shrugged. "Hadn't been for you," he corrected, "I would have been swinging from that hoist beam."

The woman stirred tiredly, glanced about the barren, dusty interior of the cabin. "You won't ever know for sure now about your brother."

Starbuck made no answer. He had began to prowl the room like a restless, caged animal, searching for a way to freedom. There was but the one door, he saw, and he'd waste no time or energy trying to break it down. Not only was it secured by a hasp and blocked by a timber propped against it, but Blackjack Johnson's three hired hands would be close by, ready to shoot him down should he succeed in opening it.

There were glassless windows high up in two of the walls, but both were small, little more than ports. Bunks had been built into the sides of the structure, and in a back corner a table arrangement had been constructed with a shelf above it. There were no other furnishings of any kind.

Starbuck paused, hearing the sharp crackle of fire. Almost at once, wisps of smoke began to filter in through cracks in the nearby wall and floor. He stood rigid, listening, thinking, racking his brain, hearing the quick tread of boots—probably Pete Dawson—hurriedly circling the shack as he spread the flames to the tinder he'd banked along the sides. Within only a very few minutes the place would be ringed with fire, and it would take but moments more for the sun-bleached lumber to explode into a holocaust.

Rose had begun to cough as the smoke thickened steadily. "What—what can we do?" she managed between gasps.

There was a note of fear, of desperation in the woman's voice now. Previous to the moment, she had seemed to accept what lay ahead for them with an offhand, almost amused resignation. But that had vanished as the fire began to mount.

The floor . . . Starbuck swore quietly at his own

stupidity. The joists, resting on a foundation that consisted only of rocks piled at each of the four corners, raised the wide planks a foot or more aboveground. If he could manage to pry up one of the boards . . .

Immediately he reached into his boot, drew out the knife he carried there, and going to his knees, began to examine the floor at the rear of the shack. The planks had been jammed tight together in the interest of keeping out the cold, but he finally located a narrow space between two of them, and brushing aside the dust to find the nearest nails, thrust the blade of his knife into the crack and began to pry.

Smoke now filled the room with a thick, heavy fog, and the crackling of flames was much louder. The front wall had caught, was beginning to blaze, and shortly, he knew, the rear and remaining side would catch and go up.

"Shawn . . ."

Rose had seen what he was endeavoring to do, had moved in beside him. She was coughing and choking, and tears were running from her eyes.

"Can I help?"

He shook his head, worked steadily at the boards as sweat poured off his face and his eyes also smarted and wept from the acrid smoke. The boards had been nailed tight, were refusing to loosen. Leaning closer, he put more weight on the knife's handle. He heard the planks creak, give slightly, and hope surged through him. He bore down on the knife more heavily. The blade snapped like a dry twig.

An oath exploded from his tight lips. He withdrew the weapon. The blade had broken off midway. The part near the hilt was thicker, stronger than that which had snapped. Hunched on his knees, gagging, feeling the increasing heat, he forced the stub in between the boards. Outside, the flames had begun to roar and the smoke had thickened to the point where he could scarcely see what he was doing, but he kept doggedly at his task.

"Hurry, Shawn—hurry!"

Silver Rose's plea was like spurs raking his sides as he crouched over the knife. He had less leverage now with the shorter blade, but he could exert more pressure. The boards groaned again as the nails began to pull loose. They gave an inch—two—three. Hope again filled him. He jerked the knife clear, laid it aside, wedged his fingers into the cracks, and grasping the board, endeavored to raise it.

The nails stubbornly refused to release. At once he pivoted, glanced at the makeshift table, barely visible through the choking haze. A length of wood serving as a leg supported its outer corner. Crossing the room in a single stride, he wrenched it free.

Wheeling, he returned to the loosened floorboard, and knuckling his streaming eyes in an effort to see better, jammed the arm-long bit of lumber into the narrow opening he had managed. He paused then, looked at Rose. A tight grin parted his lips.

"Maybe," he said, and threw his weight on the pry.

For a long, breathless moment the nails held, and then gave suddenly with a loud, protesting squeal. Instantly there was a blast of hot, smoke-filled air from the draft created. Ignoring the searing wave, Shawn pushed the plank out of the way, beckoned to Rose. There was barely enough room for them to slip through, gain the ground beneath the shack, but it had to be done.

"Going to be a tight squeeze," he gasped. "And there'll be fire."

The woman, coughing, face tear-streaked, managed a smile. "Anything'll beat getting roasted in here," she said, and began to force herself through the opening in the floor.

He nodded, said, "Start crawling toward the back. I'll be with you in a minute."

Wheeling, he crossed to the opposite wall, and standing on the bunk built against it, he peered through the window. Smoke, boiling about the shack, was so dense he had difficulty in locating Dawson and the others, but finally, with heat scorching his skin and smoke filling his lungs and stinging his eyes, he saw them.

Immediately he leaped to the floor and hurried to the opening. In very few minutes the shack would be a solid mass of flames. Fire had already broken through two of the walls, was climbing upward and licking greedily at the roof.

Rose was under the house, flat on her stomach, waiting. He dropped down beside her. Smoke had gathered in the area beneath the doomed structure, but it was not yet as dense as it was inside and the heat was less noticeable.

"Stick close to me," Starbuck said, and began to work his way toward the rear.

With each succeeding foot, as they drew nearer to the flaming wall, the heat changed, became more intense, but it would be foolhardy to delay, hope the fire would lessen. The cabin was a tinderbox and no part of it would escape complete destruction.

Shawn reached the end of the joists. Through the rolls of smoke he could see the blackened embers of the weeds Dawson had used to start the fire. Above the still smoldering ashes was the thick timber used as a support for the wall. It, too, was black, and the edges glowed brightly from the flames roaring above it. Starbuck turned to Rose.

"Keep that scarf covering your hair," he said hoarsely. "Once we're past that beam well be all right."

The woman nodded woodenly, and Shawn, pulling his hat low, inched forward until his head was even with the beam. Then, propelling himself with the toes of his boots, clawing at the dry, blistered soil with his fingers, he thrust himself into the open.

Turning quickly, ignoring the hot sparks and ashes dropping upon him, he knelt, and reaching in under the smoldering timber, caught Silver Rose by the hands and dragged her into the clear.

CHAPTER 14

COUGHING, GAGGING, SUCKING DEEP FOR FRESH AIR, Starbuck sank to the ground beside the exhausted woman. The shack was now a seething mass of flames and billowing smoke, and the heat was intense.

He turned to her. Small coals smoldered in her dust-covered clothing. Leaning over, he pinched them out. Face streaked with sweat and soot, she managed a tight smile and sat up.

"Was mighty close," she murmured.

He had not escaped the touch of fire either. There were burned places in his shirt, his hat and pants, and from some, tiny, thin streams of smoke were curling. He smothered the small, glowing circles with a thumb and forefinger, and then removing his bandanna, gave it to her.

"Use this," he said.

Rose began to wipe at her face and neck as she glanced toward the roaring flames. "What do we do now?"

Shawn got to his feet. "First thing—move. Pete and the others are on the other side of the shack. One of them could take a notion to come around, have a look."

Reaching down, he took the woman by the hand, assisted her to rise. Immediately she began to brush herself off. He looked about.

"Can see a ditch over there," he said, pointing to a slight berm some yards distant. "Probably was dug for drainage. You can wait there for me."

Frowning, Rose paused. "What are you going to do?"

"Got to get the horses . . . and a gun. No point in holding off. Looks like that ditch runs all the way across the back of the town. If it's deep enough I can get down in it, crawl to the last of the shacks, and circle in behind Pete and them."

"Do you know right where they are?"

"Took a look through the window just before we got out. Were all sitting on a bench somebody'd built in front of one of the shacks, watching the fire."

"But what can you do?" Rose asked, alarm lifting in her eyes. "You don't have anything to fight them with, and they're all armed!"

"I'll find something," Starbuck said. "Let's get over to that ditch."

Taking the woman's hand, he struck out across the uneven, littered ground, halted when they reached the canal. It wasn't as deep as he'd hoped, but by lying down, Rose could keep out of sight, and unseen by Blackjack's men, he could move the length of what a number of hopeful souls had planned to be a settlement.

The flames of the shack were beginning to die, and

84

within a few more minutes the structure would become nothing but coals and ashes. Whatever he was to do before that moment came, must be done quickly, Shawn realized; the men were certain to rouse themselves and have a look around to reassure themselves that no evidence of the fire's victims remained. Too, his best chances for over-coming them lay while they were together.

As Rose seated herself in the ditch, he walked to a pile of cans, bits of wood, and other debris on beyond her a half-dozen strides. Poking about in the mound, he came up with a broken pick handle. It would make a good weapon until he could get his hands on a gun.

Returning to Rose, he nodded, said, "Want you to keep down until I come for you. If it happens I don't make it back, stay hid until it's dark. Good chance you'll be able to get away from them then."

The woman smiled soberly. "I think you'll be back," she said quietly. "Good luck."

He grinned, dropped to a crouch, and moved off along the ditch. For the first few yards he was hidden from the clearing that would have been Hangdog's main street by the irregularly spaced shacks, but when he came to an open space between the last of the structures and the one preceding it, he was forced to drop to his knees.

He could see Dawson, flanked by Hawken and Sugarman, still on the bench, and as they were only partly turned away from him, he deemed it wise to take no risk of their catching motion from a corner of an eye and glancing in his direction.

Bent low, sweating freely, Shawn quietly worked his way across the open strip to the end shack, standing apart from the others short distance. Once there and behind it, he drew himself upright with a grunt of relief.

The muscles of his legs were screaming from the strain the unaccustomed position had placed upon them, and he paused, allowing them to ease. But the need for urgency pressed insistently at him, and gripping the pick handle, he moved along the weathered wall of the shack until he was at the corner, facing the haze-filled street.

The backs of the three men were to him. A grin of satisfaction pulled at Starbuck's long lips as that became apparent. But closing in on them to where he could make use of his club was not going to be easy. He would be in the open all of the way, and the smallest sound made by him would draw their attention instantly.

There was no alternative. Grim, he glanced down, checked his person for any part of his clothing or equipment that might betray him. He had removed his spurs back in Goldpan and put them in his saddlebags, thus there was no worry there. He could find nothing else that was in need of silencing, turned his attention back to what lay ahead. It would simply be a matter of a slow, cautious approach, aided, fortunately by the deep, cushioning dust in the street and the crackling and popping of the diminishing fire.

It was best he keep low, he decided, and delaying no longer, pick handle gripped tightly, he stepped out from the shack and started down the street. At that moment a portion of the burning cabin's roof gave way, fell with a crash. There was a crackling of flames and a shower of sparks, and smoke shot upward. Starbuck reacted instantly. Taking full advantage of the noise, he quickened his stride.

"I reckon that about does it!" Pete Dawson's voice reached him as he drew near.

"Still got a little burning to do," one of the others

countered. "We don't want nothing left."

"That's for sure," Chaw Sugarman agreed. "And that's got me to puzzling—what about the buggy and them horses? What're we going to do with them?"

The words being spoken by the men were clearly audible to Starbuck as, crouched low, pick handle raised to strike, he closed in.

"Buggy ain't no problem," Dawson said. "Can burn it, too. Horses are something else."

"Why not sell them?" Hawken suggested. "Ought to bring a big price."

"Don't know nothing about the sorrel," Chaw said, "but there's a lot of folks around here that'd spot that black mare of Rose's. We dassen't try selling it in any town in this part of the country."

Starbuck, barely breathing, his movements as slow and studied as those of a stalking cat, eased in silently. Another step . . .

"We'll trot them across the line into California, that's what we can do," Dawson said. "Be nobody over there that'll know who they belonged to."

"Unless that Starbuck come from over that way."

"Nope, don't think so. Looks like he was from cattle country."

"That's going to take time," Hawken said, shaking his head. "Blackjack said we was to be back in town by dark. Wants folks seeing us standing around and . . ."

"It won't make no difference," Pete cut in. "Us getting the job done is what he wants. Now, you and Chaw can take them horses and sell them. I'll ride back to town, let Blackjack know everything's fine and dandy. Bragg's been covering for us, and I'll side him, make it look like we're all there. Anybody asks about you two I'll just say you're around somewheres."

"But that ain't what Blackjack—"

"I'll do some explaining to him. It'll be all right."

Hawken spat, scratched at his whiskers. "Why can't you drive them horses over and sell them, let me and Chaw go back to town?"

" 'Cause it makes more sense was I to."

Starbuck drew himself fully erect. Linus, starting to make a protesting reply, broke off abruptly as he caught motion from the tail of an eye.

"What the hell!" he shouted, and lunged to his feet.

CHAPTER 15

STARBUCK SWUNG THE PICK HANDLE IN A SHORT, swift arc. It struck Hawken on the side of the head, sent him staggering into Dawson and Sugarman as they leaped upright.

"Goddammit," Pete blurted, struggling to regain balance and draw his pistol.

Shawn, making the most of surprise, crowded in, flailing at both men with the length of oak. He knew he had only moments; the pick handle would be no weapon against a gun.

Dawson yelled as the club smashed him across a forearm. Reeling, cursing, he fell back, dropped his pistol. "Get him!" he yelled to Sugarman, on his knees and bringing up his gun.

Starbuck lashed out with his foot, buried the toe of his boot in the balding man's body. Chaw groaned, recoiled, but managed to get off a shot. The bullet ripped through the slack in Shawn's pant leg. He rocked to one side, swung his club at Sugarman's head. The blow was low. It connected with the man's shoulder, the driving force of it knocking him over.

Starbuck, pivoting and taking a long, plunging step, reached the prostrate and senseless Hawken. Pete Dawson, holding his arm, was bending over, trying to retrieve his fallen weapon, apparently forgetting the one he had earlier taken from Starbuck and thrust under his belt.

Shawn kicked out again, sent a spray of dust into Pete's face and all but burying the gun the dark-faced man sought to recover. Dawson swore, hesitated, and Starbuck, seeing Sugarman again leveling for a shot, wheeled, swung the pick handle once more in a wicked, whistling half-circle.

This time the stout bit of oak found its mark. There was a sickening thud as it met Chaw Sugarman's head. The man came half upright, yelled, went over sideways, and sprawled full length.

Starbuck, sweat soaked, dust swirling about in yellow, flat layers, spun to face Dawson. Pete, still holding his arm, was legging it for the nearest shack. Shawn lunged forward, bent over the quivering Sugarman. Reaching down, he seized the man's pistol, wrenched it from the stiffening fingers that held it, and came back around. Dawson was just disappearing behind the abandoned cabin.

Taut, Starbuck moved to follow, doing so warily. Pete was certain to realize he had a pistol, make use of it, and Shawn in no way intended to set himself up as an easy target.

Eyes narrowed to trim the glare, breathing hard for wind, he walked slowly toward the shack. Dawson could be inside if the sagging old structure had a door in its back wall. He doubted that. Most were hastily built affairs similar to the one in which Silver Rose and he were supposed to die, and if true, Pete Dawson would be hiding behind it. And he would not seek safety on the slope lying beyond; there was nothing there to offer shelter—only low, ankle-high weeds.

Starbuck gained the corner of the shack, halted, listened. Somewhere off on the hillside a meadowlark whistled, the cheerful note strangely out of place in that small universe of heat and shifting dust and drifting smoke.

Shawn drew up sharply. The dry sound of cloth scraping against wood had come to him. Immediately he rushed across the front of the shack, turned down its short wall, and pistol ready, hurried to the rear. The solid thump of boot heels brought a curse to his lips. Wheeling, he doubled back to the street. Dawson was nowhere to be seen.

"Shawn . . ."

It was Silver Rose. He swung about to face her. She was standing near the blackened ruins of the still smoldering shack in which they had been trapped.

"Pete—he's over there—inside," she called, pointing to the cabin at the end of the street.

The blast of a pistol echoed hollowly from the hut indicated by the woman. The bullet splintered a board in the shack just beyond Starbuck. Dawson had discovered the weapon he was carrying. Shawn jerked back, again circled the small structure, and trotted to its rear corner. Pete had closed the door of the cabin where he'd taken refuge, was firing from one of the windows.

Taking a deep breath, Starbuck snapped a bullet at the hut, raced across the open area of the street, and hauled up against the building adjacent. Sheltered by its bulk, he threw a glance at Sugarman and Linus Hawken. Both lay where they had fallen, unconscious from the blows

90

they had taken from the pick handle. He need fear no more problems with them, Shawn reckoned, and turned his thoughts to Dawson.

Pete, forted up as he was, would be hard to reach. The advantage lay with him, as he could hold out as long as his ammunition lasted without exposing himself to return fire. A tight smile pulled at Starbuck's cracked lips. He could take a leaf from Pete Dawson's book— and would.

Dropping back, he circled in behind the shack, and kicking clumps of dry weeds and bits of trash ahead of him, wedged them against the wall and in under the structure. A few scraps of wood lay close by, the trimmings of boards cut to shorter lengths, and these, too, he gathered and tossed into the pile of tinder.

Judging he had a sufficient amount, Starbuck drew a match from his shirt pocket, scratched it into a flame with a thumbnail, and dropped it into the accumulation. The match caught instantly, but he delayed until the tongues of fire spread and began to lap at the bleached wood of the cabin's wall. Then, doubling back to the street, he took up a stand where he had an unobstructed view of the door.

Smoke began to boil up from the rear of the shack in dense, writhing clouds, and what had at first been a quiet snapping and popping grew steadily into a loud crackling. There was no sound, however, from the man inside. Starbuck remained motionless. Pete would have to make a move soon. He would be unable to withstand the heat and smothering smoke for much longer. It could be. . .

"Damn you, Starbuck."

Shawn whirled. Linus Hawken, leveled gun in hand, was on his feet. He had misjudged the man, but it was no time for censure. Buckling, pivoting, he fired his weapon. Hawken got off his shot in that same fragment of time. His bullet went wide. Starbuck's, triggered fast but with care, drove into him, sent him reeling backward, blood spurting from his chest as he went down.

Shawn, tense from the close call, wheeled to face the now furiously blazing shack in which Pete Dawson was hiding. In that same instant the door flung open, and Pete, firing as he came, lunged into the open.

Starbuck flinching as a bullet seared across a forearm, squeezed off two shots in rapid succession, swore as the weapon clicked on an empty cartridge. He took a quick step to the side, fingers pressing out shells from the loops of his belt—hopefully of the same caliber as the gun he was using.

In that next moment he saw there was no need for haste, or to reload. Pete Dawson lay facedown in the dust, arms outflung, legs spraddled.

For a long time Starbuck stood quiet in the streaming sunlight, powder smoke drifting about him while flames raged through the nearby shack, heating the already stifling air and filling it with bits of ash and glowing sparks. Finally his shoulders lifted, and he walked slowly to Dawson.

Tossing aside the pistol he'd taken from Sugarman, he recovered his own weapon from where it lay near the man's stiff fingers, and rodding out the spent cartridges, refilled the cylinder with fresh shells and dropped the weapon into its holster.

Turning on a heel, he crossed to Linus Hawken, had his look at the man . . . dead. Pivoting, Shawn moved on to Sugarman . . . dead, also. Shaking his head wearily, he continued on down the street toward Silver Rose, hurrying to meet him.

CHAPTER 16

"YOU ALL RIGHT?" THE WOMAN ASKED, STUDYING HIM anxiously.

Starbuck shrugged. "Couple of scratches," he said in a toneless voice. He did not mention the several small burns, now an angry red, on his face and hands. "How about you?"

"Scorched," she replied indifferently.

She, too, had numerous burns, but she was ignoring them. She had managed to remove some of the soot from her face; there were still dark patches here and there on her arms and neck, and her hands looked as if she had been in the coal bucket.

Obviously relieved with his answer, she turned, glanced at the lifeless bodies beyond him. "Poor Pete," she murmured. "And Linus and Chaw. Blackjack just used them, and they were too dumb to see it."

Starbuck's jaw hardened. "Got what they bargained for. They were out to kill us."

"I know—and you're sure as hell right. It's only that Blackjack's a great one to get others to do his dirty work, and they usually end up like Pete and Chaw and Linus Hawken—dead. But this bungs the barrel for me. Makes me realize I've got to settle with Blackjack before he gets another chance to put me in a pine box. You still not interested in doing the job for me?"

The grimness and tension was, at last, beginning to drain from Starbuck. Shuttered eyes on the burning shack, now almost down to embers, he said, "No, reckon not."

"Well, I'll get somebody else. Sure looking forward

93

to seeing Blackjack's face when I walk through the door. . . What're we going to do with Pete and them? Can't just leave them laying there."

Starbuck glanced about, ducked his head at one of the remaining structures. "Put them in there, close it up tight. Coyotes and buzzards won't be able to get at them. Can send somebody back for the bodies when we get to Carson City."

"Could bury them right here if we had something to dig with."

"Can't spare the time," Shawn said bluntly.

Silver Rose frowned, and then understanding came to her. "You're thinking about the killer—Lindeman's."

"Him, and some others. Can bet we'll have to deal with them yet, and if they're on the road behind us—and ahead, too—they'll be closing in."

She nodded. "I keep thinking there's only the one in the blue shirt to worry about."

"I'd like to believe that's the way of it, but I doubt it. We saw only two men back in Goldpan, but if it was important to somebody to want Lindeman dead, then I can't see them leaving the job up to only a couple of guns."

"And now that they've got Amos, they're out to fix me so's I can't talk. I sure ain't enjoying all this popularity: my husband trying to kill me on one hand and them on the other!"

"Can cross out your husband."

"Helps, got to admit that. I never was one to back off from trouble, but I'm sorry now I got a look at those killers."

Starbuck grinned wryly. "For my part, I can't say I am."

Rose smiled back. "That's the only good side of it."

Shawn had turned, was now staring off in the

direction of the road. There was no telltale, yellow pall in sight. Satisfied, he swung his glance back to the haze-filled hollow of Hangdog.

"Time we pulled out. We got lucky, outsmarted Dawson and his two friends. With a little more of the same luck maybe we can outsmart the killers that are looking for you. Go wait in the buggy. I've got a couple of chores to take care of."

"I can help."

"No, nothing you can do, and we ought to keep an eye peeled for dust, back of us and on ahead, too. Sing out if you spot any."

"All right," Rose said as he turned away and moved off to where Pete Dawson lay.

Taking the man by the heels, Starbuck dragged him to the nearest of the shacks and laid him inside. He turned then to Sugarman and Hawken, followed a like procedure, after which he collected their weapons and tossed them onto the floor beside the bodies.

Shutting the door, which had been stripped of its hasp, Shawn used the length of wire hanging in its stead to hold the panel in place. Studying the twisted wire critically, he doubted its ability to withstand the persistent efforts of coyotes, and bringing up what was evidently intended to be a post in a projected fence, he wedged it securely against the door.

Brushing at the sweat blanketing his face and misting his eyes, Starbuck wheeled and crossed to the buggy. Rose was waiting for him on the seat.

"No sign of anything," she said as he swept the horizon with a quick glance.

The three horses ridden by Johnson's men, tied to a rear wheel of the vehicle, were standing hipshot alongside the sorrel. Starbuck stepped up to the first, retrieved his rifle, and laid it in the bed of the buggy.

"What'll you do with those horses?" Rose asked. "If we leave them here, they'll starve . . . or die of thirst."

Shawn was already at the nearest, stripping it of its saddle and bridle, dropping them in a pile to one side.

"Not much we can do but turn them loose," he replied, moving to the next animal and beginning to remove its gear. "Like as not they'll follow us when we pull out."

He finished with the second horse, hurriedly went to work on the last "Bound to be a creek or a spring around here somewhere—and where there's water, there'll be grass."

Rose frowned, thinking deeply. "There is a creek—I remember now. . ."

"Where?" Starbuck asked, without pausing.

"Not sure," the woman replied, looking around. "I'm sort of mixed up—lost—being off the road like we are, but seems to me it's about halfway between Goldpan and Carson, maybe a bit farther."

"Means it's still on ahead of us then," Shawn said, climbing up and taking his place beside her. "We hadn't come to it yet when that bunch stopped us."

"That's right."

"Probably a couple of hours on down the way," Starbuck said, taking up the reins. "Ought to reach it about dark."

"If we don't run into another bunch waiting for us along the road between here and there," Silver Rose said wearily, and settled back.

CHAPTER 17

STARBUCK WAS RIGHT ABOUT THE THREE HORSES. They had stood motionless, heads up, ears pricked forward, watching as the buggy, trailed by the gelding, rolled off; then, impelled by sudden intuition and as if on signal, all broke into a run and quickly caught up.

And when Shawn, near sundown, drew in under a lone sycamore growing in a swale through which a shallow creek flowed, they were trotting contentedly alongside the sorrel. At the smell and sight of water, however, they forsook the big gelding's companionship and raced up to the small stream, where they eagerly slaked their thirsts. Watching them, the mare and the sorrel both whickered anxiously.

Climbing down from the vehicle, Starbuck surveyed the couleelike area. It apparently was a place used frequently by pilgrims, both for resting and for overnight stops. The black scars of numerous camp fires were in evidence, and there was a pile of dry wood and a makeshift shelter of brush.

"It's late," he said, glancing to the western horizon. "As well spend the night here."

Rose nodded tiredly. She was showing the strain of the long, hot, tension-filled hours.

"I'll have to see to the horses first, so you sit easy," Starbuck added. "Soon as they're taken care of, I'll fix us a bite to eat."

"Can't I do something to help?"

Again he refused her offer of assistance. "No, it's a man's job."

She shrugged her full shoulders and stepped down

97

from the buggy. "Then I'll take time and do a little cleaning up," she said, and moved off toward the creek.

Shawn made no reply, and unhitching the mare and releasing the sorrel, he led both down to the stream and allowed them to ease their thirsts. It had been a hard day for both, and he permitted them only a few deep swallows and then took them back to the buggy, where he tethered both to a rear wheel.

Filling the nose bag partly with grain for the mare, he hung it in place; he poured a quantity onto a bit of canvas he found in the bed of the vehicle and laid it on the ground for the sorrel; then he turned to his saddlebags and carried them into the camp area.

The stray horses had wandered off along the creek, where grazing on the thin grass found along its banks and Rose, sitting on a rock a bit this side of them, was washing herself as best she could with her handkerchief.

Drawing some of the blackened stones scattered about into a three-quarter circle, Starbuck built a fire from the wood, conveniently available, and filling the lard tin he used for making coffee from the stream, he set it over the flames.

That much toward a meal begun, he dug into his grub sack for the food he had on hand: a small amount of bacon, three potatoes, and several hard biscuits. Slicing the meat and potatoes into the frying pan he carried, he placed the spider over the fire alongside the tin of water. Scattering a few of the biscuits, dampened to soften them, along the circle of rocks, he then joined Rose at the stream to do a bit of cleaning up himself.

When they returned to the camp a time later, the water had begun to boil in its container and the mixture in the frying pan was sizzling busily. Starbuck, setting the lard tin off the fire, added a handful of crushed

98

coffee beans, allowed the beverage to surge up, and then stirring the froth to settle it, reached for the cup he'd placed nearby.

"Got only one of these," he said, filling the container and handing it to the woman. "I'll drink mine from the tin."

Rose smiled. "Smells good, but I expect a mite of whiskey'll help," she said, and going to the buggy, returned shortly with the bottle of liquor. Pouring some of the coffee back into the lard tin, she refilled her cup with whiskey and handed the bottle to Starbuck.

"Luck," she murmured, and raising the cup to her lips, had a long swallow.

Starbuck, matching her drink, turned to the mixture in the frying pan, stirring it with a spoon taken from the grub sack. The bacon was cooked, but the slices of potatoes were still hard, and half turning, he gathered up a handful of dry branches and added them to the fire.

"I just ain't got over Blackjack screwing up enough sand to get me killed," Rose said. She had seated herself close by, was staring into her cup.

"From what you've told me it's not hard to understand," Starbuck said dryly.

She looked up considered him briefly, and then nodded. "Yeh, guess I have been sort of twisting the knife in his guts. Losing out on the Lady Luck and having to stand by and watch me run it to suit myself galls him plenty, but he ain't got no squawk coming. It was all on the fair and square."

"Doubt if he keeps that in mind."

"Can bet he don't! There ain't nothing you can tell me about Blackjack Johnson that I don't already know—in spades."

Shawn looked off into the closing darkness. "You

said something about him being surprised when you walked in the door, after you've been to Carson City. Not likely. He'll know something went wrong when Dawson and the other two he sent to kill you don't show up."

"Been thinking about that," Rose said, adding, more whiskey to her cup.

"There a chance he'll be gone when you get there?"

The woman shook her head. "Not Blackjack. Be like him to bull it out. There's only one way I'll ever get rid of him, and that's kill him."

The concoction in the spider was ready. Starbuck divided it, scraping half into the tin plate he carried, surrendered the spoon to Silver Rose, and using the jackknife he had in a pocket, ate his portion directly from the pan. The biscuits had softened only slightly, but they were warm.

When the slim meal, eaten in silence, was over, Starbuck refilled Rose's cup from the tin, and both sat back to enjoy the last of the whiskey-laced coffee before retiring for the night.

"Be a big help if Blackjack would take off before I get back . . . figuring I do get back," Rose said, picking up the earlier topic of conversation. "He's smart enough to know I'll be gunning for him."

Shawn, staring into the dwindling fire, made no comment.

"And that's what I'll sure be doing—gunning for him," Rose declared. "When somebody's out to kill you, smart thing is to beat them to it. In this world the first rule is to stay alive—survive—and I've managed to do that ever since I was a kid."

The last of the coffee was gone. Starbuck set the lard tin aside, got to his feet. Silver Rose would do exactly what she planned and, undoubtedly, when it was all over, the Lady Luck would still be hers; she was that kind of a woman.

"Expect you'd best do your sleeping in the buggy," he said, glancing at the horses. "Can use my blanket."

A look of concern crossed her face. "Where'll you be?"

"There, under the tree by those bushes," he said, pointing. "Want to be where I can keep an eye on things."

Rose gave that thought while she slowly drew herself erect. "That means you figure there's a chance we might have some company."

"No way of knowing. Just don't believe in taking anything for granted."

She nodded. "I appreciate that. . . You turning in now?"

"Soon as I picket the horses down along the creek," he replied, and moved toward the rear of the buggy. "Good night"

"Good night," she answered, and watched him lead the mare and the sorrel off into the pale darkness.

CHAPTER 18

STARBUCK WAS AT MUCH LESS EASE THAN HE exhibited to Silver Rose. He slept lightly and intermittently, shoulders against the springy bulk of a currant bush, the rifle across his knees. Several times he roused, to walk quietly out of the camp and from the slightly higher point of a nearby knoll search the moonlit land with a probing glance.

He could not pin down the precise reason for the

disquiet that filled him; it was not the certainty that men involved in the killing of Amos Lindeman were seeking them; that was a foregone conclusion. It was something more definite, more tangible—as if he and Rose had already been overtaken and the killers awaited only a convenient moment to strike.

Yet his periodic examinations of the adjacent road and the area surrounding the camp revealed no riders moving in from any direction. Too, the coyotes and other creatures of the night continually made their presence known, which was an indication that there was no one abroad. But Starbuck was unsatisfied, and when the first streaks of dawn began to color the eastern sky, he felt a flow of relief.

Propping the rifle against the trunk of the sycamore, he set about getting a fire started. Refilling the lard tin with water, he placed it over the flames and again delved into his grub sack for the morning meal. There was a little bacon left and the last of the biscuits.

Crushing the circular bits of bread into small chunks, he dumped them into the spider, added the chopped bacon and a quantity of water, and put the combination on the fire beside the tin. Rising, he moved off to have a look at the horses.

The sorrel and the black mare had grazed to the limits of their ropes. Both appeared rested. The three horses that had followed them from Hangdog had wandered some distance on below, and in the crisp, early light he could see them cropping grass along the banks of the stream.

Dousing his head in the cold water, Starbuck returned to camp, found Rose, the blanket draped about her shoulders, bottle of whiskey in one hand, huddled near the fire. She looked up, smiled, offered the liquor to

102

him. He accepted, had himself a short drink, then put his attention on the simmering contents of the frying pan.

"Seen you up walking around a couple of times during the night," the woman said. "You hear somebody?"

Shawn shook his head. "No, just making sure we wouldn't get surprised. Expect it was hard sleeping in that buggy."

"I've been through worse, but I was so damn tired I never noticed. The horses do all right?"

"Fine," he replied, and added coffee to the water in the lard tin.

Rose looked off in the direction of Goldpan. "Maybe nobody's following us, after all. Seems, if there was, they would've caught up by now," she said hopefully.

"Like to think so, and the same goes for on ahead, but we sure can't bank on it. I remember you saying this camp spot was halfway or so to Carson."

"Seems that was it."

"Means we've still got some traveling to do before we can breathe easy," Starbuck said, and filling the tin cup full of steaming coffee, handed it to the shivering Silver Rose. "Here, get this down. It'll warm you more than that whiskey will."

Rose set the bottle aside, enclosed the cup with both hands. "I never have been able to understand how this country can get so damned cold at night and still turn hotter'n hell in the daytime."

"Way the desert is," Starbuck said, removing the skillet from the fire. "Reckon this stuff's ready."

Taking up the tin plate, he spooned out a generous half of the mixture, passed it to her. She placed her cup beside the bottle of liquor, and grasping the spoon, began to eat at once. Shawn, again using his pocket knife, went to work on the remainder.

"It's hot, if nothing else," he observed.

"That's what counts with me right now," Rose said, and then hastily added, "not that it don't taste mighty good."

The sudden crackle of gunshots cut into her words. Bullets spurted sand a few yards in front of them, clipped through the trembling leaves of the sycamore.

Dropping the spider, Starbuck lunged to his feet, reached for the rifle leaning against the trunk of the tree. Snatching it up, he jacked a cartridge into the chamber. Dropping to one knee, he leveled the long gun at four riders racing toward them at full gallop, firing as they came.

"Get down low!" he shouted at Silver Rose, and drawing a bead on the man slightly ahead of the others, pressed off a shot.

The rider buckled, threw up his arms, and fell from the saddle. At once his companions veered off, realizing the short range of their pistols was no match against a rifle.

Starbuck, rising quickly, hurried to one side, hoping to get a line on another member of the outlaws, but they were quickly behind the crest of the low hill down which they had come, and out of sight.

He turned then to Silver Rose, dusting off her clothing as she slowly came to her feet.

"Guess there ain't no doubt about it now," she said ruefully. "There's some folks that sure want me dead!"

Starbuck, reassured of the woman's well-being, had swung his eyes back to the hill beyond which the riders had disappeared. They'd pull up there, he reckoned, decide their next move. Likely they had rifles and would make use of them when they tried again . . . and he'd no longer have an advantage.

The man he'd knocked from the saddle lay unmoving in the short weeds, apparently dead. His horse had trotted on toward the creek, evidently in search of the water he could smell, and being thirsty could mean the outlaws had been riding hard the entire distance from Carson City.

"Guess you were right about them getting the word from the telegrams Henry Deveau sent," Rose said. The bottle of whiskey was again in her hand. "Must've started that bunch out right away to head us off."

"No doubt about that," Shawn said, still watching the downed man's horse. It had located the creek, was now taking its fill of water in long, sucking drafts while the black mare and the sorrel looked on from the opposite bank.

"Now we got them—and blue-shirt and maybe a couple of friends he's scraped up to help—coming at us, front and back. Guess we're caught in that squeeze we were talking about. Chances for getting to Carson City are slimming down, unless you've got some good ideas."

Starbuck shrugged. "Only one—get the hell out of here somehow."

"I'm sure in favor of that!" Rose said with feeling, and fortified herself further by taking another drink. "What I can't figure is how."

"Expect that bunch up there behind the hill are going to sit back now and wait for blue-shirt and whoever else he's lined up to help come along. Intended to take us by surprise themselves—and they would have, only they misjudged the range of their pistols. Think I'll have a look, see if I can make out for sure what they're up to. Best you keep down."

Rose nodded, and Shawn, carrying the rifle, doubled back up onto the flat above the hollow where the camp lay. A wash, twisting in from the higher plains offered possibilities, and dropping into it, he hurriedly made his way to a point where he could see the far side of the rise behind which the outlaws had taken refuge when he opened up on them.

He caught sight of them a few minutes later, hastily dropped to a crouch. They were off their horses, and squatted on their heels, were engaged in discussion. Getting near enough to hear what was being said was out of the question, of course, but undoubtedly it concerned Rose and him and what further measures should be taken.

Narrowing his eyes to cut down the rising glare, Shawn studied the outlaw's horses. He could see no rifles on the saddles of two, but the third, a chunky buckskin, was turned broadside to him and he was unable to tell if there was a long gun in a boot slung from its hull or not. But he would bear the probability in mind; if the men made another attempt to charge the camp, he'd train his sights on the buckskin's rider, for he could be the only one with an effective weapon.

The outlaws seemed in no hurry to make a second charge, however, and that could mean reinforcements from Goldpan were expected. Their logic was understandable; why risk getting shot when they need only to hold off, allow blue-shirt and his party to arrive, and move in from the opposite side of the camp, which would then become a trap rather than a fort?

He couldn't let it come down to that, Starbuck decided. He could probably stand off three men by taking advantage of the campsite area, but with a second group coming at him from behind, he'd not last long.

There was but one answer: get out fast and head for Carson City. That was easily said, not so easily done, he realized, turning his attention to the country before him. It rolled out long and flat, with only small knolls here and there to break the sameness. The high mountains, which could offer cover and allow them to pass unseen, were all far in the distance.

Below the camp, downstream, could lie salvation. There was brush growing along the banks of the creek, not in thick or in great profusion, but enough to offer a degree of concealment..

Unacquainted with the area and unable to see for any length because of the stream's winding course, he could not tell exactly what to expect; but, regardless, it appeared to be their one chance for slipping out of the hollow beneath the sycamore and avoiding what most certainly could turm into a death trap for Silver Rose and himself.

Wheeling and still careful to keep low, Shawn trotted back up the wash for camp. If the creek proved to afford no means for escape and their movements were detected, it would come down to a shootout between him and the three outlaws. With the odds all against him in such event, he still preferred that to being caught in the crossfire of two parties, where he'd have no chance at all.

CHAPTER 19

"DID YOU SEE THEM?" ROSE GREETED HIM ANXIOUSLY as he slipped into the swale.

Starbuck nodded. "They're just sitting up there behind the hill. Pretty sure they're waiting until help comes from Goldpan."

"Just what I was afraid of. Scheme is to catch us in between them, squeeze—"

"Not if I can help it," Shawn cut in, looking off downstream. It was a narrow, meandering ribbon in the now strong sunlight.

Rose frowned, stirred wearily. "I don't see that we've got a choice other'n—"

"Always a choice of some kind," Shawn said, gaze still on the creek.

From this different angle he could see that it bore west despite an erratic course. The brush did not appear to play out, and it looked as if anyone keeping in the water between the two lines of growth would be effectively screened. However, from the side of the hill where the outlaws were waiting, it could be another story; movement along the stream might be clearly visible, but it was a risk they would have to take.

"We don't have much time," Starbuck said, coming to a decision. "No way of knowing how close the bunch from Goldpan are, so we best get out of here fast. Even if we're wrong about it and there's no help on the way, we'll be fools to stay here. Sooner or later those jaspers'll get the idea of splitting up and coming at us from three sides, and the odds are all in their favor that we won't be able to hold them off. . . . You think you can set a saddle?"

Rose nodded grimly. "I can do anything that I have to."

"That mare saddle broke?"

Again the woman nodded. She wasn't questioning him about the buggy, pressing for reasons why they couldn't continue using it, he noticed, and that pleased him. They were faced with a critical situation, and he would have had little patience with her had she complained about the discomfort of riding horseback.

"I'm going down and get the horses," Starbuck said then, his voice showing urgency. "Won't take but a few minutes; be ready to go."

"I'm ready now," the woman replied. "Can save time if I go with you."

"Need to have a look at that hill where they're hiding first. Not sure if they can see this end of the creek—and the horses. If they can, we've got more trouble."

Two rapid gunshots abruptly rolled across the flat. A bullet dug into a low sandbank close by; another struck a rock near the buggy, ricocheted, and went screaming off into space. Starbuck, about to move off, glanced at Rose, nodded tautly.

"Guess that proves they've got a rifle . . . and that they're waiting for somebody."

"You don't think they're going to try and rush us again? If you do, give me your pistol. I can use it."

"No, they just threw those bullets at us to let us know they were still there . . . and that we're pinned down. Just set tight."

Stepping out from under the sycamore, Shawn glanced toward the hill. The rifleman was not in sight, had evidently crawled to the crest of the rise, triggered his two shots, and pulled back to rejoin his friends.

Hunched low, eyes switching back and forth from the uneven ground before him to the hill, he hurried on. So far the lower end of the formation stood between the outlaws and the creek, blocking off their view. It was possible they were paying scant attention to that area, he realized, were concentrating their efforts on the camp and Silver Rose's buggy. While the sycamore tree prevented their looking directly into the coulee, the vehicle was out where it could be seen with no difficulty.

He came to the sorrel and the black, dozing in the mounting heat. The horse belonging to the outlaw he had shot had crossed the stream, and as if seeking companionship, was near the mare.

Starbuck paused, studied the distant hill closely. He could not see the men, and unless the rifleman chose to return to the crest to fire more warning shots at the camp, he could get to the animals and, unseen, lead them back to where Silver Rose was waiting.

And the stream would provide a means for escape, he saw, throwing a final glance down the twin bands of growth with their dividing strip of sparkling water. He need not worry about being seen, once they had gained the first of the brush; their one danger would lie in crossing a short strip of open ground on below the horses.

Too, he could still tell but little about the land farther on, for vision was yet limited to the first hundred yards or so, but that was something they would face when they reached it. The point now was to get the horses and gain the brush.

The black would need gear. That occurred to Shawn as he brought his attention back to the animals. Rose could never manage to stay on the mare without a saddle and bridle, and it would be fatal to burden the sorrel, big and strong as he was, with two riders. They would be making a hard, fast run for a considerable distance once they reached a safe distance downstream, and the gelding, handicapped by the extra weight, would fall short of doing his best.

He wished now he'd had the foresight to bring along the gear from Pete Dawson's horse or one of the others, but it had never entered his mind that they might have use for it. The outlaw's bay horse . . . already equipped, he could solve the problem for Rose. But the bay appeared worn, and Carson City, so far as Starbuck knew, was many miles to the north. The bay would never stand up under a continual ride, but he was the source for the necessary gear.

Shawn threw another glance at the hill. There was no one in sight, and hurrying out from the mound of weedy earth behind which he'd halted, he circled in behind the horses. Taking first the trailing reins of the bay, he then collected those of the black and his sorrel gelding, and led them back to the camp. Rose, as earlier, was anxiously awaiting him.

"Can we make it?"

"Chances are good. We'll ride down the middle of the creek . . . may have to get off and wade a few times if the brush peters out. Only problem's going to be getting to the water. Some open ground to be crossed."

He had brought the horses in close to the sycamore, looped their lines about the squat bushes at its base, and was already hurriedly unsaddling the bay.

The quiet was again shattered suddenly by two quick shots from the crest of the hill. The horses jumped at the sound, and Starbuck swore softly as he hung tight to the bay's bridle.

"Telling us again that they're there," he said. "They can see your buggy and they keep laying bullets around it, and that's good. Long as they can spot it, they'll figure we're here."

Rose had stepped up to her mare, was holding to its rope. "Wondered why you were bringing along an extra horse . . . can see why now."

"Going to be a hard ride, if we make it out of here,"

Shawn said, pulling the saddle and blanket off the bay and swinging them onto the little black. "Be quite a chore staying aboard without some gear."

"Specially for me," Rose admitted. She was in good spirits despite the precariousness of their position. "Been a long time since I was up on a horses back."

Shawn cinched the saddle into place, and without bothering to measure, hastily shortened the stirrups a few inches. Stepping up to the bay's head, he slipped the bridle and bitted the black. The headstall was too long for the mare, and he had to release the buckle, reduce the strap's length a bit. It took extra time, but he felt it was necessary; better to make an such adjustments now than later, when to stop could be costly.

"You're ready," he said then to Rose, and turned to the sorrel.

It took only a moment to tighten the gelding's cinch and put the bridle, removed and hanging about the red's muscular neck so that he might graze easier, back into position. Picking up his rifle, Shawn slid it into the boot and smiled tightly at the woman.

"Let's move out"

Rose immediately swung the mare about. "We mount up?"

"No, got to lead them horses till we reach the brush," Starbuck said, and holding the sorrel's lines, moved off.

Gaining the edge of the hollow, he glanced at the hill. There was no one visible. If the rifleman intended to lay shots around the camp at regular intervals, it should be another ten minutes or so before he fired again.

Walking fast, Shawn led the way to the point where the horses had grazed, halted. Nodding to Rose, he pointed to the first line of brush a short distance on ahead.

112

"Once we're there, we'll be all right. The risk is getting to it. Pretty sure we can be seen by them while we're crossing over."

"Still a better deal than staying here and getting ourselves all shot to hell," Rose said in her flat, matter-of-fact way.

Starbuck was staring off to the south. A cloud of dust was hanging in the motionless, hot air. Someone was coming up from the direction of Goldpan. It could be pilgrims on the road, a stagecoach, freight wagons, or it could be blue-shirt and more outlaws coming to join those waiting on the yonder side of the hill. If it were the latter, they were moving out none too soon.

"I'm agreeing with you on that," Starbuck said grimly. "Keep up alongside my horse. If they spot us and start shooting, mount up and make a run for it—right down the middle of the creek."

Silver Rose considered his taut features thoughtfully. "You're not giving much for our chances, are you?"

"Not much," he said frankly. "Was no way of finding out if they could see us once we got out in the open."

"You'd likely be doing this different if I wasn't along, wouldn't you? Not hard to see that running from them goes against the grain."

Starbuck shrugged. "Odds are a bit long."

"Doubt if that would bother you. Expect you'd figure out a way to get to the top of that hill, trim the odds somehow, and have it out with them."

"We're wasting time."

"Guess we are, but I wanted you to tell you I pretty much know how you feel and that I appreciate what you've done and are doing for me, in case I don't get another chance to say it."

"You do what I told you and you'll make it through,"

113

Starbuck said, casting another side glance at the distance roll of dust.

"I'm to make a run for it if they start shooting at us. What about you?"

"Aim to slow them down a bit with a few shots. You just keep riding north. Carson City's up there somewhere. You won't need me to show you the way. Let's go."

CHAPTER 20

STARBUCK HALTED AT THE EDGE OF THE CLEARING, eyes on the hill. So far the rifleman had not made an appearance. He beckoned to Rose, a stride to the rear.

"Keep going," he said in a quick, taut voice. "When you reach the brush, ride. I'll be right behind you."

Without hesitation Silver Rose stepped out in front of him, leading the mare. She looked neither right nor left, but, wholly intent, entered the open ground and with firm, rapid steps, started for the brush.

Starbuck, rifle in one hand, the leathers of the sorrel in the other, moved to follow, but his eyes were not on the sheltering channel of the creek, but on the hill. If the outlaw presented himself again with the intentions of firing more warning shots at the camp, he'd not fail to see them.

Too, they could be hurrying into full view of the men. Each stride they took carried them farther out of the blind area created by the hill itself. But so far, one-third of the distance, the outlaws were still hidden, and they, accordingly, from the men. It just could be luck was with Silver Rose and him, and they'd make the crossing unnoticed.

Shawn swung his gaze then to the south. The yellow, misshapen ball of powdery dust looked larger, closer. Whoever or whatever, it was coming on fast. From the size of the ball it could very easily be a stagecoach, but he knew he could not depend on that; four or five horsemen, riding hard, would churn up a like cloud.

He brought his attention back around. Halfway . . . He glanced then to the hill. No sign of the rifleman or his two companions, but one of their horses could now be seen. The blocking shoulder of the hill was dropping away. Within only a few more yards the point would be reached where he and Rose would be in view of the outlaws.

Three-quarters of the way. Starbuck could see all three men now. Two were sprawled out on the warm sand; the third—the rifleman—was resting on his haunches, weapon across his knees. He was turned partly away. A tiny streamer of smoke from a cigarette or cigar was trailing upward from his mouth.

Shawn became aware that Rose had halted. He glanced to her, saw her grasp the horn of the black's saddle, thrust a foot into the stirrup, and draw herself up onto the hull. The woman made no sound, simply drummed her heels against the reluctant mare's ribs to force her off the bank and into the creek. A moment later, water spurting out from under the horse's hooves in small, flat sheets, she was moving in between the twin lines of brush.

Starbuck mounted his sorrel immediately, flung a final glance at the hill as the big gelding stepped down into the stream in the wake of the black. The outlaws had not stirred, were yet totally unaware that Silver Rose and he had abandoned the camp. He grinned tightly, urged the sorrel, showing his dislike for the

115

spray of cold water striking his muzzle by continually jerking his head, to a faster walk. They had made it.

His spurs were still in his saddlebags, and he was wishing he'd taken time back at the camp to strap them to his boots. Later, when he had an opportunity, he would. The moment could come when he'd be forced to press the sorrel for his best.

He drew up close to Rose. Features strained, she turned to him, looked on beyond saw that they were well along in the channel. A smile of relief parted her lips.

"They didn't see us. We got away."

Shawn nodded. "Haven't missed us yet, either."

She raised herself slightly in her stirrups, considered the land ahead. "How far do we follow the creek? It's heading west and we have to go north."

"Need to put some distance between us and the hill before we cut away and start bearing for Carson City. Things've all gone right for us so far, don't want to press our luck too hard. . . . Having any trouble with that saddle?"

"Doing fine," the woman replied, and settled back.

The brush was thin, somewhat scattered. Starbuck continued to keep watch on the hill. The outlaws could possibly see them if they suspected they were there and looked closely, but a casual glance would likely reveal nothing.

They pressed on steadily, following the winding stream as it continued westward. Shortly, Shawn could no longer see the outlaws as a rise in the land now intervening shut them off. At that same moment the distant, flat crack of the rifle reached them once more. Rose smiled back at him over a shoulder.

"Guess that proves we've made it; they think we're

116

still there in the camp."

He nodded. "And we've moved out of sight. Can get back on dry land and head north now."

Rose swung the black away from the creek bed, hammering on the little mare's ribs again with her heels to make her break through the wall of brush and gain the open ground beyond. As Shawn kneed the sorrel in beside her, he pointed into the distance.

"That's north. Carson City's there somewhere."

"How far?"

He shrugged, swiped at the sweat on his forehead. "I'm guessing, but I'd say it's at least twenty miles. Could be a bit more."

Rose smiled tiredly. "Guessing is all I could do. I'm so turned around now I don't know where we are, but it seems we ought to be closer than that."

"It's a two-day ride from Goldpan, and I'd say we've been on the move for more than half that when you tot up the times we've been at it."

She sighed, changed her position on the saddle, which was evidently already tiring muscles unused to hard leather surfaces. "I hope it's not much farther."

Gunshots again floated hollowly to them—not from the direction of the hill, but seemingly more to the west in the area below the camp. Shawn cut the sorrel about. None of that was in view, but the dust pall, nearer than before, was all but gone. Rose saw it then for the first time.

"That cloud—"

"Been watching it, Came up from Goldpan. Could be the bunch those outlaws were waiting for."

"Then they've met."

"Likely, and the shooting could mean they've made a run at the camp—this time from two sides. Won't take long for them to find out we're not there and start looking around." Starbuck paused, leveled a finger at the lower end of a mountain range well in the distance. "Smoke there. Probably Carson City. Point for it"

Rose waited no further, and once more using her heels on the mare, sent the horse rushing up the slight incline rising before them and out onto a broad flat. Shawn was close behind.

The big sorrel quickly drew abreast of the mare, and then, side by side, they struck off across the level land at a fast gallop. Looking ahead, Shawn saw that there would be no relief from the open country. There were no hills, not even of small size, nor could he see any indication of arroyos that might permit them to drop below the level of the surrounding plain and avoid being silhouetted against the skyline.

He held the headlong pace for a good half-hour, and then, as he felt the sorrel begin to slacken, drew him down to a slower lope. The black, striving to match the gelding stride for stride, immediately followed suit, and they continued on toward the ragged line of blue-gray mountains, which seemed no nearer.

They would have to pull the horses in to an even slower pace, Starbuck knew, but he was anxious to get as far from the hill and the campsite as possible before doing so. The heat, which had been rising rapidly with each passing minute, was now beginning to tell on the animals. Flecks of foam were coming from their muzzles, and dark patches of sweat were showing up on the mare's black coat.

A solitary upthrust of weed-covered earth and rock took shape a distance ahead. Starbuck leaned toward Silver Rose.

"We reach that we'll pull in for a time. Can't afford

to run the horses into the ground!" he shouted.

The woman nodded. She had one hand on the horn, raising herself slightly off the saddle to lessen the solid impact of the black's hooves meeting the firm soil. That she was suffering was evident, but she was making no complaint.

The mound drew near, much larger in size than expected. They came even, swung around to its far side, and halted. Both horses were blowing hard, and their coats were stained with sweat. Shawn and Rose, too, were showing the effects of the driving heat, and both came off their saddles at once, not only to lessen the load on the horses but also to get relief from clothing plastered wetly to their bodies.

Rose, moving away from the heaving animals, began to fan herself with a soiled handkerchief. High overhead in the burning sky a half-dozen vultures were soaring lazily in broad circles. She shuddered.

"Those damn things always give me the chills," she murmured.

Starbuck, moving about the horses, examining them carefully, paused, followed her glance. A hard smile pulled at his lips.

"Long as they stay up there I don't mind."

She seemed not to hear. "It's like they know we're not going to make it and are just hanging around . . . waiting."

The raspy sucking of the horses for wind had ceased, and now both were standing quiet. But the black showed signs of the hard run. Starbuck, procuring his spurs from the sorrel's saddlebags and affixing them, eyed the trembling mare critically. He doubted that the horse had another such run left in her. Despite her sleek, well-cared-for appearance, she, like an athlete who had neglected training, had gone soft and had little stamina. They would need to take it much slower for the next few miles, give her a chance to recover. He reckoned now they would have been better off with the outlaw's horse.

"Time we moved on," he said, turning to the sorrel. "Well have to go easy on the horses, rest them again after a bit."

Wordless, Rose crossed to the black, pulled herself onto the saddle, stiffened. Starbuck, too, had come to sudden attention. Both had seen the roll of dust at the identical moment.

A half-dozen riders, indefinite in the heat-filled, shimmering distance but outlined clearly, were racing across the flat toward them.

CHAPTER 21

STARBUCK, ABRUPTLY TAUT, UNACCOUNTABLY angry, leaned over, slapped the black smartly on the rump. Startled, the mare leaped forward. As the horse rushed off with Silver Rose crouched over the saddle, one hand clutching the horn, the other gripping the lines, he raked the sorrel with his rowels and veered in behind her.

Almost immediately the mare began to lag. Shawn swore deeply. The little black would never make it. Although the sorrel, accustomed to long days of hard traveling, could easily outdistance the outlaws' horses, undoubtedly tired from the miles already covered, he would have to ignore the advantage and keep himself in between Rose and the outlaws.

Twisting around, he looked over his shoulder. The

riders had gained slightly. Seven men, he saw. That meant four had come up from Goldpan to join the trio waiting on the hill . . . and blue-shirt was one of them.

The people who wanted Amos Lindeman dead and had succeeded in bringing it about were apparently not only well organized but determined as well. Little wonder the U.S. marshal and other authorities in Carson City were anxious to bring about an identification. Unquestionably well financed, a ruthless group such as they were dealing with, if allowed to go unchecked, could virtually control the state's government.

The sorrel, running smoothly, was closing the gap on Rose and the black, but Shawn could not be certain if the mare was slowing even more or if the gelding's long legs were narrowing the distance. He began to veer the sorrel away from the black, avoiding the dust lifted by her pounding hoofs, and glanced ahead. There was nothing but the empty land. The faint smudge of smoke they were pointing for in the distance, however, was growing more pronounced.

He tried to gauge the distance as they raced on. Ten miles? Fifteen? It would be nearer the latter, he reckoned, considering the distance they had put behind them when compared to the halfway position of the campsite on the road. But it was of little consequence— could as well be a hundred miles, for the black mare was wilting fast under the hard pace and the murderous heat.

Grim, Starbuck impatiently brushed sweat from his eyes with a forearm. It was beginning to look as if he'd never reach Virginia City. That struck him as ironical. After all the years of searching for Ben, and with the conclusion of the quest undoubtedly awaiting him there, an outlaw's bullet seemed likely to prevent it.

And if Ben were dead—and the note to Arlie Bishop from Virginia City's sheriff had stated he was dying—then all the time and effort, all the years put into the search would have gone for nothing. The last of the Starbucks would disappear with their deaths; finish would have been written to a family.

He became aware that Silver Rose had turned toward him. Her features were tightly drawn, glistening with perspiration. Seeing that she'd caught his eye, the woman shook her head in a sign of hopeless resignation. That they would never make it to Carson City was evident to her, also.

He forced a grin, nodded encouragingly, and yelled, "Keep going!"

But he knew that to do so for much longer would be impossible for the mare. She'd given her best. Now her strength was fading and she was going on heart alone.

Starbuck cast a glance at the outlaws. They seemed no nearer, had fanned out into a forage line, but were not losing ground, either. Their horses-big, tough, hard-muscled animals like the sorrel—were no strangers to strain, and even if worn, could still give a good account of themselves.

He looked again ahead—to the direction in which Carson City lay. The smoke plumes were more definite, now much thicker. The settlement was within Silver Rose's reach if the black mare could slack off, rest for a bit. He reckoned that was the answer; that opportunity would have to be provided.

The flat, he saw, throwing his gaze about, was slanting, funnellike, to a lower level. The land appeared to be breaking up, and here and there small, ragged washes, in which the infrequent rains drained from higher ground, were evident.

Bent low over the pounding sorrel, hopes lifting, Shawn sent his eyes probing across the plain. A distance farther on, near the base of a low bluff that was taking shape, there looked to be a somewhat larger and deeper arroyo. He could see the tops of brush clumps and the flat shine of rocks as they reflected the sun's relentless rays. His hopes increased. The cut offered the one chance he sought that would allow Rose to reach Carson City. Urging the sorrel to a longer stride, he caught up with the black. The woman turned her despairing features to him. He pointed at the arroyo.

"Aim to pull up in there . . . want you to keep going!" He was shouting to be heard above the thunder of the horse's hoofs.

Rose frowned, shook her head. "No. I'll stay. I can shoot a gun . . . help you."

"Not what this is all about. It's important you get to Carson."

She bit at her lower lip, released her grasp on the saddlehorn, and wiped at her eyes. "I—I don't think my horse can go much farther."

"She can if you slack off, take it slower. Reason why I'm pulling up, making a stand. I'll hold that bunch off until you get a good lead, then I'll follow."

Rose studied him thoughtfully. Finally, "Is it the only way?"

"Only way," he shouted back. "They've got to come down off the flat, pass by that arroyo. I'll stop them there."

She was not fooled. "There's half a dozen of them— more, actually. You can't hold them back alone."

"No big chore," he replied. "Arroyo looks pretty deep. It'll be like a fort. When we get to it, you ride on, but let the mare slow up. Point for that smoke in the sky.

123

Carson City's there."

They had reached the slope, were beginning the more conspicuous drop-off to the weedy land below. Starbuck slowed the sorrel, allowed the mare to forge ahead while he had his look at the oncoming outlaws. They had gained ground. It was fortunate the arroyo was near. He'd have just enough time to pull up, get himself set.

They reached the foot of the grade, rushed on. Shortly they came to the edge of the wash—dry, fairly wide, and studded with sagebrush, rabbit brush, and scattered rocks. As the mare went off the bank, she stumbled, caught herself, and almost staggering, hurried on with the sorrel only a length behind her.

Midway across Starbuck pulled up, swerved toward a large clump of brush. As he threw himself off the saddle, dragging the rifle from its boot as he did, he saw Rose look back. Her dust-streaked face was sad as she smiled, raised her hand. Starbuck gave her a responding wave and wheeled to meet the outlaws.

They appeared at the top of the slope almost immediately, all moving together to make the descent where the horses of riders in the past had converged and pounded out a narrow trail. They could see that Silver Rose was out of the arroyo and on the flat beyond it, he knew, but the fact that he was no longer with her apparently had not registered on their consciousness as yet.

Crowded together at the top of the grade, they would have made easy targets for Starbuck as he crouched low in the center of the wash, but he withheld his fire. To open up on them at that point could cause them to separate, scatter across the high ground that overlooked the cut, and put him at a disadvantage. He wanted them where they could not turn back.

Methodically Shawn mentally ticked off the riders as their horses, stiff-legged, blowing, leather squeaking, descended the slope. Through the boiling dust he could make out their bearded, set faces. He recognized none of them other than the blue-shirted one who had made the attempt on Rose's life. He was third in the line.

A yell went up from the outlaws. Someone had realized that the woman now rode alone. Starbuck drew himself partly erect, looked in her direction. She was no longer visible to him because of the rise in the land beyond the arroyo, but she would be well on her way. Turning back, he again faced the oncoming riders and raised his rifle. It was time to bring them to a halt. Sighting on the outlaw in the lead, he pressed off a shot.

As the shocking echoes bounced along the arroyo, the man threw up his arms and spilled from the saddle. Shouts filled the hot, dusty air, and the remaining riders split apart and spurred off into the ragged growth.

Deliberate, Starbuck drew a bead on another of the outlaws, squeezed the trigger of his rifle. The man clutched at his chest, tumbled from his wildly plunging horse. . . . Two down, but the last shot had given away his position. A hail of bullets hammered at the weeds and rocks behind which he was crouched.

He lunged forward and, prone, wormed his way nearer to the bank of the arroyo. Bullets continued to slash the mound where he had been, and the smell of powder smoke began to hang in the deep wash. Careful, he pulled in close to the low, rooted wall, and removing his hat, peered over its edge.

The outlaws were off their horses, had taken refuge behind whatever they found available: rocks piles of dirt, bushes, the stump of a dead tree. Leveling his rifle, he lined its sights on a hunched shape partly in view.

When he fired his shot, Shawn drew back hastily, once again changed location.

As before, the puff of smoke gave him away. Guns began to rattle, like a drumroll, and dirt exploded in small geysers along the rim of the arroyo, farther out in its bed, even on the opposite bank as the outlaws sought to cover him with a curtain of lead, but he was the length of a long yard from where he had been, and went untouched.

He heard the sorrel whicker suddenly. And then came the solid thud of the big gelding going down. Starbuck rolled over to get a look. The sorrel lay quivering on the sandy floor of the wash, blood spurting from his head, where one of the outlaw's bullets had found a target.

A wave of anger surged through Starbuck. There had been no need to kill the horse. He had been standing off to the side and in clear view. The fact that the bullet had struck him in the temple was proof the shot had been no stray, but intentional.

A deep sense of loss pushed aside the anger in Starbuck. The big red horse had been his reliable friend and companion for years. At the start of the search for Ben he'd bestrode one of the old farm horses. Finding it too slow and plodding, he had traded for a chestnut, and then later he'd come upon the sorrel and again made a change. They had been together from then on—through weather good and bad, times of hunger or plenty, of tension and ease, and thus had become as much a part of the quest as the object of it.

They had been as the three sides of a triangle in the search: Ben, the sorrel, and himself. Now the sorrel was dead. Ben, also, if he accepted as fact the letter received by Arlie Bishop from the sheriff in Virginia City. Thus he alone remained of those involved in the long, tedious

126

quest.

And he was not but a breath away from joining them. In halting the outlaws so that Silver Rose might escape safely, he had trapped himself. He had known that from the start and accepted it, and while he would have the satisfaction of exacting a high price from the outlaws, they eventually would get themselves organized, come at him from two, perhaps three sides, and that would be the end of it.

But it wouldn't matter then. Rose would have reached Carson City, or be almost there, and the outlaws would have no chance to overtake her. She would be able to identify the men who had killed Amos Lindeman, and the law, taking its course, would halt the attempt of greedy anarchists endeavoring to claim the state for their own selfish purpose.

The faint crunch of gravel somewhere behind him brought Starbuck around swiftly. A shadow rose from behind a thick clump of rabbit brush. Shawn triggered his weapon. The outlaw fired in the same fragment of time. Starbuck felt the numbing shock of a bullet as it ripped into his arm, heard the crackle of branches as the man toppled and fell.

It was blue-shirt. Starbuck grinned tightly. At least he'd made the killer of Lindeman and Caleb Green pay up for his crime.

He looked down at his left arm, hanging limply at his side. The bullet had entered the fleshy part just above the elbow, leaving a deep gash in its searing passage that was bleeding profusely. He hadn't been aware of it, but he'd let the rifle fall when he was hit, and now, painfully using his right arm, he picked up the weapon and, shoulders braced against the wall of the arroyo, laid it at his side.

He was out of it now, he reckoned. A left-handed man, he was awkward and had little skill with the right. But it wasn't in him to quit. Pulling his bandanna from around his neck, he stuffed it into his shirt sleeve to where it was bunched against the wound, and then, reaching across his body, drew his pistol. The rifle was now useless except for firing the shot in the chamber, but he could still manage a hand gun.

Literally back to the ragged wall of the arroyo, he waited for the outlaws to close in. The smell of dust and powder smoke was still thick in the motionless, heated air, and off down the wash a gopher broke the quiet with its quick staccato bark. He glanced again at the sorrel, stiffening in the sun. It was odd, he realized, but he'd never given the big gelding a name, simply called him "horse" or "sorrel."

Starbuck stirred uncomfortably. His wound was paining, now that the anesthetic of shock had worn off. Why the hell didn't they move in and get it over with? The odds were all on their side now, but they seemed reluctant to make a move. It was so quiet a man could think they were no longer there, had pulled out.

"Starbuck! Starbuck! You all right?"

A hard grin split Shawn's dry lips. He struggled to draw himself upright, turned his eyes toward the opposite bank. A soldier wearing lieutenant's bars was looking down at him.

"I'll make it," he called back.

Elsewhere other soldiers, off their saddles, were filtering into the arroyo, and under the guidance of a hoarse-voiced sergeant, were rounding up the remaining outlaws.

"How bad are you hit?"

The young officer had come off the bank, was now

128

facing him. Starbuck shook his head. "Not too bad, I reckon. Like to know where you came from?"

"Was a bit north of here with my patrol. Met a woman—Rose, she said her name was. Told us what was going on, that you were here holding off a gang of outlaws. Asked me to help."

"She all right?"

"About done in for sure. Had a couple of my men take her on into Carson. Glad we got here in time."

"Goes double for me, Lieutenant," Shawn said wearily.

CHAPTER 22

VIRGINIA CITY STILL BORE THE SCARS OF THE DIS-astrous fire that had ravaged it a few years earlier, Starbuck saw as he rode slowly down one of the lesser streets of the settlement, sprawled at the foot of the ragged, barren mountains.

But there was new construction in evidence everywhere, and it was apparent the holocaust had done little damage to the spirit and ambition of those living in the famed Comstock Lode country. The towering, six-floored International Hotel looked down upon a hundred busy saloons—chief among them the Delta, the Sazarac, and the Bloody Bucket—countless stores, restaurants, mine-supply establishments, and a dozen or more huge, rambling ore mills with their tall smokestacks funneling dirty, gray clouds into the sky.

But Shawn paid scant attention to such. After the arrival of the soldiers, a patrol under the command of a young lieutenant of about his own age, whose name he learned was Cantrell, he had appropriated one of the

129

dead outlaws' horses and ridden on into Carson City with them and their prisoners.

There his wound had been attended to by an army physician who also prescribed a few days' rest. Starbuck had given little heed to that also; he had met with Silver Rose that night, listened to the details of how her identification of the killers had made it possible for the U.S. marshal and other police authorities to move in on the combine of men behind the murder of Amos Lindeman and take them into custody; and he had ridden on that next morning, despite her entreaties to lay over for a few days.

The matter of his brother was now, more so than ever, foremost in his mind, and no amount of discomfort and pain was going to prevent his making the ride to Virginia City from the Nevada capital now that he was so near.

If Ben were dead, then the search was over and he could begin a new life—one that only hours earlier he had thought was at an end. But luck had favored him and now he was, or could be, facing the culmination of all those days and months and years of endless drifting and numberless, bitter disappointments.

The sheriff,s office was near the end of the street, he had been advised, and looking ahead along the teeming roadway, crowded with hurrying people, heavily loaded wagons, buggies, shiny black surreys driven by liveried chauffeurs, and saddlemen, he located the sign hanging above its door.

Guiding his horse, a stocky, barrel-bodied black gelding, through the crush, he picked his way to the narrow, barred-window structure, and turning into the hitch rack, drew to a halt. Dismounting, a tense sort of expectancy building within him, he secured the black, and crossing the board sidewalk, entered.

A bearded man in corduroys glanced up from the desk at which he was working over a report.

"Yeh?"

The jail apparently lay beyond the door in the rear wall; a prisoner confined to one of its cells could be heard singing in a loud, off-key voice.

"You Sheriff Halverson?"

The bearded man shook his head. "Nope. Name's Craig. I'm a deputy."

Starbuck felt the edge of his keen anticipation dull. Had he come up against a blank wall again?

"Is Halverson still around?"

Craig studied him thoughtfully. "Out of town. There something I can do for you?"

A sigh of relief slipped through Shawn. "Maybe so. I'm looking for a man named Friend . . . Damon Friend. The sheriff mentioned him in a letter to the marshal of Tannekaw, over New Mexico way."

The deputy clawed at his beard. A man somewhere in his forties, he had a deeply pocked face and a large, veined nose.

"Friend? Can't say as I recollect any such fellow, and I been here going on to five year. Who'd you say that marshal was?"

"Didn't say, but his name was Bishop. Letter to him said Friend was in a hospital here, dying of gunshot wounds. I don't know how long that was."

Outside in the street a freight wagon rumbled past at excessive speed, the driver standing up shouting to pedestrians and others in an effort to clear his way. Craig rose, stepped to the door, and looked out, his glance angrily following the vehicle.

"Damn honyocker," he muttered, and came back

131

around. "What was the name of that fellow you're looking for again?"

Starbuck stirred patiently. "Friend. Damon Friend. He—"

"Yeh, seems I am remembering somebody by that handle," Craig said, reseating himself. "What're you asking about him for?"

"He's my brother," Starbuck replied, hoping he wouldn't have to go through the story again. The difference in names always started lawmen to wondering and asking questions as to why Ben had changed his name.

"Yeh, Friend. I recollect him. Got hisself shot in a holdup . . . only it turned out he didn't have nothing to do with it, just got caught in the crossfire."

Shawn leaned forward, features taut. "Did he die?"

The prisoner in the jail had been joined in song by a fellow inmate and the sound of their raucous voices began to fill the small office. Craig got to his feet again, crossed to the inner door, opened it.

"Shut up, dammit!" he yelled, and as the song hushed abruptly, he closed the panel and returned to his chair. Lowering his head, he began to study the papers strewn about on the desk.

"What about Friend?"' Starbuck persisted, holding tight to his temper. "Did he die?"

Craig raked a finger through the tangled burnside of his left cheek. "No; matter of fact, he didn't. Got all right."

Shawn settled back, relief flowing through him again. Ben, at least, was alive.

"He still around here?"

"Hell, I don't know," the deputy snapped peevishly. "Lot of people in this town nowadays. I can't keep track

132

of everybody." He hesitated, frowned. "Do recollect seeing him once or twice. Been a spell, however."

Starbuck shrugged as resignation took over. Ben had not died, and he was thankful for that. But it added up to the same old story: he'd missed him again. The search wasn't ended, after all.

"You got any idea where I might look for him— around here, I mean? Where'd he live? He hang out at any saloon special?"

"I don't know nothing about him, much," Craig said irritably. "Expect he done his hanging out at all the saloons, and I sure don't know where he was living."

Starbuck nodded as the deputy once again began to work on his report. "I'm obliged to you, Craig, anyway. If he happens to show up, I'll appreciate it if you'll tell him I was here looking for him and to leave word where I can get in touch."

"Sure," the deputy said, and then glanced up, frowning. "Just come to me. Before he got mixed up in that shooting, he was dealing faro at the Red Garter. Somebody there might be able to tell you something, if you're of a mind to do some asking. It's right down the street."

Asking . . . inquiring . . . leaving word . . . That had been the pattern of his life, the rule of his daily existence for more years than he cared to remember, Shawn thought. And it was beginning all over again in the settlement where he had believed it would finish.

"Obliged to you again, Deputy," he said, and opening the dust-clogged screen door, stepped out onto the sidewalk.

Pulling back against the wall to avoid the constant flow of people, he threw his glance along the facades of the buildings on the opposite side of the street. The Red

Garter . . . He located the sign, let his eyes drop to its entrance, shadowy beneath an extending porch roof.

Shock and surprise hit him like a solid blow to the belly.

Standing in front of the saloon, leaning against one of the overhang's supports, was his brother. A broad grin parted Shawn Starbuck's lips as he brushed at the sweat gathered on his forehead.

"Ben!" he shouted, and stepping off the walk, hurriedly began to thread his way through the turmoil of traffic choking the street.

The search was over.

We hope that you enjoyed reading this
Sagebrush Large Print Western.
If you would like to read more Sagebrush titles,
ask your librarian or contact the Publishers:

United States and Canada

Thomas T. Beeler, *Publisher*
Post Office Box 659
Hampton Falls, New Hampshire 03844-0659
(800) 888-

United Kingdom, Eire, and the Republic of South Africa

Isis Publishing Ltd
7 Centremead
Osney Mead
Oxford OX2 0ES England
(01865) 250333

Australia and New Zealand

Bolinda Publishing Pty Ltd
17 Mohr Street
Tullamarine, Victoria, 3043, Australia
1 800 335 364